THE RAVEN'S SONG

ZANA FRAILLON
AND BREN MacDIBBLE

Old Barn Books

AN OLD BARN BOOK

First published in the UK by Old Barn Books Ltd 2022

Old Barn Books Ltd
West Sussex
Follow us on Facebook, Instagram or Twitter @oldbarnbooks

Email: info@oldbarnbooks.com
Web: www.oldbarnbooks.com

Distributed in the UK by Bounce Sales and Marketing Ltd
Sales@bouncemarketing.co.uk

ISBN: hardback edition: 9781910646816
paperback edition: 9781910646854
eBook ISBN: 9781910646861

Cover and text design by Joanna Hunt
UK typesetting and design by Sheila Smallwood
Printed and bound by CPI Group (UK) Ltd, Croydon, CR0 4YY

First UK edition

1 3 5 7 9 10 8 6 4 2

Here at Old Barn Books we are big fans of writing from Australia. Visit
our website to discover more award-winning and bestselling Australian
authors, including Paul Jennings, Carnegie-shortlisted Glenda Millard
and First Nations author Lisa Fuller, whose spooky YA debut *Ghost
Bird* draws on her deep-rooted relationship with
family and the land of her ancestors.

To Mum and Dad – for magic mice, fairy trees, wishing boxes, ghosts, and the stories that made me a writer. And to all those future ancestors fighting to save the world – we hear you. –ZF

To the young hearts and minds whose beautiful stubborn optimism will change the future. –BM

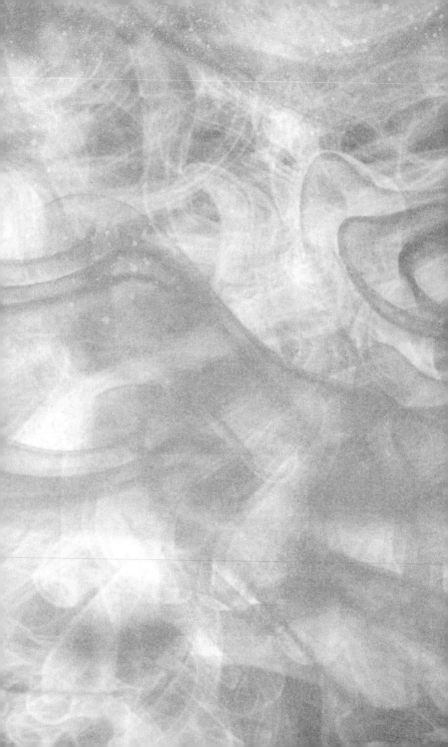

THE RAVENED GIRL OF THE BOG

(An old local folk song)

Upon one moonlit night she came
Down hillside steep and rocked
Into the place of inbetween
The Ravened Girl of the bog

Not of this world, nor of the next
In cloaks of mist and fog
She lay herself to rest in both
The Ravened Girl of the bog

Listen, listen, listen, she sang
And all through the night she spoke
In whispers long forgotten
As the souls around her woke

And in the morn they left her there
Deep down in the dark of the quag
And there she rests, and there she waits
The Ravened Girl of the bog

Never truly dead, they say
Yet never again to live
She lies and waits in waters deep
Old whispers for to give

Can you hear her as she calls for you?
Through time's great swirling fog
Listen, listen, listen …
Sings the Ravened Girl of the bog
Listen, listen, listen …
Sings the Ravened Girl of the bog.

Just once I'd like to sleep in. Just once.

There's barely a glow behind our honoured hills. The sun hardly lights my room. 'No need for curtains,' Da always says, 'coz we're up the moment our part of the world turns to the sun.' Just once though, I'd like to not be up with the sun and not coz I'm sick or nothing but coz it's nice to lie in the cool before the day heats up.

'Girl!' Da yells like he never learned my name.

'Uh?' I yell back like I never learned his.

'Girl, I need you to check the fence line before you go to school. Kashvi's lost a sheep to something.'

I haul myself out of bed and pull on my work clothes. I dunno how Da's already talked to our neighbour Kashvi and decided it's our section of fence what's got a gap, not unless Davy's already been along his section while I was lying in bed, ignoring Da's yelling, dreaming bout sleeping in. At least I'm not the only kid up to do work before school.

The door cracks open and Da pokes his head in. 'You hear me, sleepy bones?' he asks.

'Five times,' I say and give him a thumbs up.

'Good.' He shuts the door.

I wipe the sleep from my eyes and tromp out to the kitchen where Da's holding out a drink bottle in one hand and the bag with the pliers and wire in the other. I sling the bag over my shoulder and slide the drink bottle in on top.

'Nice and tight like I showed you,' he says, and musses my short hair. 'Let the chickens out on the way.'

'Uh!' I say and head out the back door, shove on my sunhat and slide my feet into my boots. I duck into the combustion loo on the way and, while I'm sitting down anyway, I do up my boots. Multi-tasking.

When I step out, Davy's hanging over the fence. 'Hey, Shel. Want me to come with you?' He looks over to the kitchen window where Da's standing. 'Kind morning to you, Mr Jones!' he yells.

'Din't you already climb up and walk your section of fence this morning?' I ask.

'Yeah, mostly with a torch. The thing woke me early, growling and roaring.'

'Like a monster?' I ask, all excited for a story.

4

'Like a lion or a tiger!' Davy says. 'I don't wanna see you go up there alone.'

'They just et a sheep,' I say. 'They won't be hungry for a scrawny kid.'

Davy laughs. 'I read that some beasts kill and store food for later. You wanna be all dead and stuffed in the crook of a tree?'

I frown. I don't think there's lions or tigers up there in the honoured jungle above both our farms, but it's still dark enough to be spooky. 'Come on then,' I say and head off across the paddock to the chicken shed. I stop to slide the door open and hens leap from the perches, squawking like they's surprised the world turned back to the sun today, and run outside into our fields in a clucking, flapping horde. It's a race to the grass, even if they was out yesterday and the day before and all the days before that in their short little lives.

We climb our hill to the tall jungle fence line that runs along the back of our property, both of us puffing a bit, sweat on our cheekbones. Ours and Davy's land being outermost this side of the township, this fence is our responsibility. If anything from the honoured and natural world outside gets in, that's on us.

Our section runs from here right down our hill to the

riverbank, where a dam controls the flow of water so we've always got some for our township. Our honoured river runs on under the fence into the wilderness. A cliff on the other side of our river follows it for ages and does the job of a fence. Anything from the natural world outside starting down that cliff will find itself smooshed at the bottom pretty quick, no matter how honoured it is.

There's a fence down on the flats, which is Mr Hajji's responsibility. It keeps the scrubland animals from coming to eat his wheat. The next township is beyond that fence line, bout two hundred and sixty kilometres south of us. I sometimes sit up here and think bout that township, wonder if there's another girl running an egg farm with her da over there. I'd like to talk to that girl one day. But two hundred and sixty kilometres is a long way to walk, even if we was allowed out there. And the doctor has the only phone on our seven hundred, just for emergencies and government business, so I can't see it ever happening.

Each township has three hundred and fifty people on seven hundred fenced-off hectares of land. No more people than that. No more or less land. These is the scientific numbers that lets the land support us and that lets us care for the land. Three hundred and fifty-one people and we start to go hungry, not if it's a little baby of course, but maybe when it gets bigger.

Davy's almost a year younger than me, his birth being approved when my ma died after I was born. Davy replaced my mother to bring the number back to three hundred and fifty, but I don't hold that against him. I guess life is hard without a mother, but life would also be hard without a best friend like Davy. And I know Davy. I din't ever get to know my mother. So when kids at school ask if I'd swap Davy back for my ma, I stomp on their toes.

'Did you have breakfast yet?' Davy asks and sits down on the hillside looking back over the township. He pulls out a lunch tin from his bag and inside is four eggy muffins full of feta cheese and veggies.

'Your mas is amazing.' I grab two and sit down in the tall tickly grass beside him. I'd be twice as scrawny if it wasn't for his mas' understanding that kids need a lot of food. Da ain't much one for cooking.

The township's waking up like a little toy town below us. The windmills turning, the cottage doors thrown open to catch the morning breeze, the flash of solar ovens being turned to the sun. The line of Mrs Nguyen's dairy cows heading out to new grass with their younger calves, and just reunited with their older calves who's galloping

7

and bucking, happy to be free after being shedded overnight to stop them being greedy little guzzlers, and her old dog Hiro making sure they all go in the right direction. Each pasture is edged by wildflowers and nut trees, like a colourful fringe on a blanket. Mrs Wang's beehive roofs is dotted through them, mostly tucked under the bigger nut trees in the shade. Her bees will be up early too, buzzing in flowers.

Our teacher, Miss Drinkwater, is outside the Walter Ticerat Community School sweeping the yard. She put in for retirement three years ago, but no word of a replacement from the government yet.

Mr Hajji leads his mules to the water trough and fetches their harnesses. Maybe he's getting ready to plant into the wheat stubble in his paddock from where it's been cut. We all got a week off school to help with that harvest. He'll stop before midday and let the mules lie bout in the shade. They's getting old, his mules, but Mr Hajji says he don't wanna train young ones so he don't mind that the government's not sent him new mules. Edith and Eddie know his land, he says, they know when to pull and when to wait patiently and it'll be a sad day when they get too old to work.

Davy points. The doctor is strolling across the field below us, heading on a direct path away from the trees around the dam back towards her house. 'Why's Dr Geraldine been to the dam so early? Me and Ma usually check the dam on Fridays.'

I shrug, and shove the last of my second muffin into my cheeks as I get up. 'Leth's find that hole,' I say around my mouthful.

We walk the fence for a while, me sucking at my teeth to get at the last of that eggy muffin, and we spot the gap from a long way off coz it's edged in white wool snagged from the sheep that got pulled through.

Normally gaps in the fence is ground level where the wire's rusted from sitting in the soil and some honoured critter's pushed up under it, but the gap we find looks like it was cut straight up in a line through the strong wire so a man bent double could push it open and squeeze through.

'Who cut it?' I ask.

Davy rattles the fence. 'Is the wire faulty?' Coz no one from our township would cut a perimeter fence, ever.

I hunt around the ground and find a couple of the links that've fallen from the fence and show Davy the wire where it's been squeezed and snipped. 'Cut!' I say.

Davy takes a link and turns it every which way and shakes his head. 'Who'd do that?' he asks. 'A perimeter fence!'

'At least we know the wild dog went back through.' I point at the clumps of wool on the wire and the blood smears either side of the fence.

Davy nods, checks out the fence up close and plucks some dark yellow fur and some black fur. 'Tiger.'

''Twasn't no tiger, Davy. Ain't no tigers round here.' I set to work with the pliers, wrapping new wire round and round to close up the gap between each link. 'The honoured and natural world is native animals only. A tiger in there with all them fat wild fowls and critters and things? Government would've hunted it down with drones a hundred years ago when the fences went up.'

Davy shakes his head. ''Twasn't no wild dog that drug a whole sheep up this hill and through this fence. This bit of land is different to what you read in schoolbooks,' he says. 'This bit's fenced off from the honoured and natural world. It don't connect to the rest.'

'How do you know?' I ask.

'I saw it when I went into the dam to help Ma clear the township water supply. There's a fence that connects near the dam fence. Not just any fence, it's real tall with barbwire on the top and signs saying *Keep Out*.'

'Why would that be?' I ask.

Davy shrugs. 'I dunno. I tried asking but no one

knows. Ma made me promise to never go in there and when I asked her why, she said, "Could be all manner of dangerous beasts in there." Like tigers, Shelby Jones.' Davy makes his eyes wide and lifts up claw hands. 'Tigers!'

A gust of cool air whispers out of the honoured trees and licks at my throat. I wipe it off with the back of my hand before it sets me shivering. 'She's just trying to keep you from getting in trouble by poking around in the good and natural world,' I say. 'She knows you's a sticky beak.'

Davy gives me a shove in the back for my cheek. Then he goes all quiet and pulls himself up against the fence, staring off up the trail made by the sheep getting dragged into the honoured jungle. 'Yeah? If this is part of the honoured and natural world, what's that?' Davy pokes a pointing finger through the fence links.

The wind gusts cool again, making the jungle leaves swish like something's brushing against them, making my hot skin goosebump.

I look where he's pointing, deep into the shadows under tall glossy-leafed trees that don't grow anywhere else on our seven hundred or on the other borders.

Tied around a tree is a wide white ribbon with a posy of wildflowers stuck through it. Dangling from them, spinning on a string in the breeze, is a disc-shape thing

11

bout as wide as a saucer with a hole in the middle. The sun bounces off its shiny mirror surface, making rainbows slide and flitter over the leaves all around it. Me and Davy twist our heads, chasing the darting rainbows as they vanish and start up new back at the disc.

'Wow!' Davy whispers.

There's a raven standing next to Phoenix's bed. A giant raven, big as a man. It's wearing bright red sneakers, and is holding a black candle and a dripping wet sack. At least, Phoenix *thinks* it's a raven. He only got a quick glimpse before snapping his eyes shut tight, but it has one white feather right on top of its head, and Phoenix has never seen a raven with a white feather before, so maybe it isn't a raven at all. To be fair, he has never seen a man-sized raven before, or a raven in sneakers, or a raven carrying candles or sacks, so the feather is probably, on the whole, not so important.

The raven leans closer, nudging Phoenix with its beak. Phoenix tries not to move, tries to pretend he's deep, deep asleep. If he's asleep, the raven will leave him alone. He'll take his candle and sack of whatever's wriggling and dripping and go back to wherever it came from, and Phoenix can tell himself it was just a dream. A hallucination even, brought on by the everyday stresses of being twelve. Giant ravens are *not* real. Logically, it makes no sense. Those wings could never lift a body that big, not to mention finding shoes to fit over those claws – but dreams and hallucinations don't drip, and this one is making Phoenix's head quite wet.

Just keep still and it will go away … The raven does not go away. It stamps its foot and snaps its beak and the air cracks like lightning, the noise growing to a rumbling, and the whole house shudders.

Phoenix sneaks a glance at his little brother Walter, still fast asleep in his bed. He takes three long, deep breaths to try and calm his mind like the doctor told him to, but even as he does he knows it will do no good. It never does. Ever since he was little, Phoenix has seen and heard things that other people don't. *It's not real. It's not real* – has been Phoenix's mantra for as long as he can remember.

'Emotional reactivity to trauma,' the doctor calls it.

'Rubbish,' Auntie Josie calls it.

'Your sixth sense!' Gran calls it, and she talks about a great gift passed down through generations of their family. 'Just like your grandfather, and his mother, and her mother before her!'

But there is no gift to waking up to a giant raven in sneakers. It's just creepy. Phoenix wishes it would leave him alone and go be a gift to someone who wants it. Like his sister Ida. She's right into all that magicky stuff. But the strange happenings aren't going away, and lately, they've been coming more often than ever.

Like on Monday, when the day turned dark as night and steam rose from the kitchen floor and small specks of fire and light danced in the air around them and Phoenix was sure it was a sinkhole opening up to devour them whole. And outside, Mum stood at the window, staring in and tapping the glass, even though she's been dead for years. No one else noticed a thing. His three older sisters were all there, and they just kept chatting and making sandwiches, and after a bit the lights faded and the steam swirled in on itself and his mum turned to a smudge on the glass, and the day just went back to being a sunny, ordinary, everyday day and all Phoenix could do was tell himself over and over again, *It's not real.*

But that panicky little voice in Phoenix's head keeps whispering – *what if… what if it* is *real?* What if all *that* was the raven's doing too, steaming up the earth to get attention. What will the bird do if it's ignored for a second time? Maybe it'll send a real sinkhole so large it devours the whole house. The whole suburb. The whole city even. That would be a lot to be held responsible for. Phoenix opens his eyes and sits up, dragging his covers over his chin.

'You're not real,' Phoenix whispers very quietly.

'Probably ... I have a very overactive imagination. All my teachers say so ...'

The raven clicks his beak and turns his head to look at Phoenix with one pale, beady eye, and then turns his head again to see him from the other.

Sweat breaks out across Phoenix's face and chest and he tightens the cover across his throat. 'Just a little, probably?' The raven jiggles the muddied sack and nods sharply and Phoenix nods quickly back. What is he even agreeing to? He stops nodding.

'Raaaarrrrrk?' The raven leans low over Phoenix and whispers, and the noise of that bird whisper is the sound of leaves rustling and mud gurgling and rain trickling. Outside, the wind slams at the windows. 'Frrmshfrk? Bmrble!' He shakes his head and ruffles his feathers. 'Brrrbkreik!'

'Um ....' Phoenix wants to tell the bird that he can't understand. He wants to say how the wind and rumbling and shaking will wake Walter – who's only just turned four – and frighten him, so if his Birdship doesn't mind, could he stop it very kindly please and thank you. He wants to ask why a raven is wearing bright red sneakers anyway, and also, can he be careful with that candle because the wax is dripping and making an awful mess and ...

But then the raven puffs up tall and monstrous and his eyes grow dark and wide. Phoenix scrambles away. His back hits the wall. His heart slams his ribs and he can't get enough air into his lungs.

'KRRRKSHKKK ARRRRGHK!' the raven screeches and the window cracks right down the middle.

Phoenix freezes. The raven's beak is level with Phoenix's face now. The beak opens wide, and then the raven places the sack gently onto Phoenix's bed.

'KrrIsknoskyelkj.' He clicks his beak. A crackle of dry thunder booms across the sky. The raven gestures around the room and out the window, his wings spread wide like he wants to scoop up the whole city. He looks so sad. What could be so terrible as to make a giant raven cry?

The raven rests his wing across Phoenix's eyes, soft and heavy and smelling of night just before it rains. The candle crackles and dies, and the waxed smoke tangs at Phoenix's nose. The raven leans close, his breath warm across Phoenix's cheek, and everything is quiet.

When Phoenix opens his eyes, the raven has gone. Phoenix's black dressing-gown is hanging from the hook on his wardrobe, right in the shape of a man-sized bird. Phoenix breathes a sigh of relief. It was just his imagination after – oh.

There, on the bed, is the sack, wet and wriggling. And there are muddy sneaker prints on the carpet, and a singe mark where the candle wax dripped.

What will Auntie Josie say? She's very particular about her carpets. *Shoes off! Shoes off!! And wipe your feet on the mat! How many times do I have to say?*

Outside, the sky is turning that orangey red of morning. Soon the others will be awake. Soon the house will be full of breakfast-making and radio-blaring and *No telly in the morning! No screens at the table!* and kettle-whistling and feet-up-and-down-stairs-stomping and backdoor-banging and hinges-squeaking and girls-arguing and Walter-laughing and Wolfy barking to be fed.

Soon the quiet and calm will be gone and all the thoughts in Phoenix's head will jumble and rush together and Josie will bundle them all out the door because it's summer and there's no staying indoors in the summer so *get going, get going, get some fresh air into you and give me some peace for once, why don't you?* Phoenix wishes the early morning quiet would last for longer.

He reaches for his phone. If only Charlie wasn't so far away, they'd know what to do. Charlie always knows what to do. Best friends are good like that.

- **You awake?** Phoenix taps.

The ping comes back almost immediately.

- It's 4 in the afternoon here ...

> - Oh yeah. So guess what? A giant raven in red sneakers
> woke me up in the night. He tried to tell me something
> but I don't yet speak bird. He was pretty upset.
> And messy.

- Wow. That's kinda random. Even for you. Are you
sure it wasn't the girls playing a trick? Frankie?

> - I wish.

- I've only been gone three weeks and you're
already seeing giant birds! Why doesn't this stuff
happen when I'm around?! I would have jumped
on its back or something. Told it to fly me to the
moon! I bet you didn't even ask for a ride.

Knowing Charlie, that's exactly what they would have done. Phoenix glances quickly at the foot of his bed. The sack is, unfortunately, still there. And it smells. Dank and muddy and mouldy. The wet of it is seeping through the doona and onto Phoenix's pyjamas and sheets. It will leave a stain, that wet. He'll have to wash the doona and dry it and get it back on the bed before Auntie Josie sees and complains about more work and *isn't it hard enough with two jobs and looking after five kids and Gran, without adding to the washing and do you know how hard it is to wash a doona?* As though it's Phoenix's fault that a giant raven decided to pop in for a visit.

- He gave me something in a sack.
- **?!**
- I haven't opened it yet.
- **What are you waiting for?**
OPEN IT!
- Should I? It's MOVING! It could be anything!
- **You know what they say — jump off the**
cliff and grow wings on the way down!
- I don't know anyone who says that.
- **DO IT!!!!**

A piece of bogweed curls from the sack like a tentacle. Phoenix watches the sack wriggle, and his head fills with river monsters and beaks and fangs and claws ...

Walter is still softly snoring. Downstairs Gran is in the kitchen.

- **P?! Are you there?! WHAT IS IN IT?!**

Phoenix takes hold of the rope wrapping the sack shut tight.

- **P?!**

The rope is thick and rough in his fingers. He unwinds, once ...

Twice ...

- **Phoenix?**

Three times around.

The *thing* has stopped moving.

Phoenix reaches his hand inside.

'Shelby Jones! Are you a child or a shrubbery?' Miss Drinkwater says the moment I step into the Walter Ticerat Community School. Miss Drinkwater seems to put some importance on appearances. I'm unkindly wishing her replacement will arrive soon.

Kids that bothered with combs and clean clothes look at me, waiting for me to look embarrassed or whatever. Easier to stay clean if your family works the weaving loom or makes soaps or furniture. Truth is, me and Davy was so late getting down that hill after seeing that ribbon and posy and little mirrored rainbow maker on the tree, we only had time for me to change the fence-repair bag for my schoolbag, and for Davy's ma to run down to the gate to swap empty lunch tin for full, so both of us is here in our grubby work clothes, our short hair clingy and foreheads wet with sweat.

I'm annoyed that Davy's not copping it along with me,

coz he's been in his work clothes since before dawn, but I'm not bout to dob on him. Three other kids have come off food-growing holdings like me and haven't bothered to change since they fed pigs or watered cabbages. All of us standing in a row in the cloakroom for a turn to wash our hands and get nails checked by Miss Drinkwater. All of us with the same short hair, in shorts and T-shirts and dusty work boots we'll have to kick off before we're allowed into school in our socks. I run my fingers through my hair trying to flatten it in one direction. 'I can't see why it matters,' I say.

Miss Drinkwater shuts her eyes and takes a deep breath. 'Tidy body, tidy mind, Miss Jones! I can't teach an unruly mind.' Miss Drinkwater is older than my da. In mule years, she'd be older than Edith and Eddie most probbly. I think Miss Drinkwater wishes she lived in a time when folks could dress fancy and not work at all if they was rich enough. Miss Drinkwater always pulls her short hair up on one side and pins it with antique hairclips with bugs or flowers on them and she always wears an antique necklace or brooch, most likely handed down from her grandmother.

Me though, I couldn't wear precious things out in the chicken sheds. I'm co-owner of an egg farm with three hundred and eighty hens and twelve roosters. I'll never get a sibling coz of my da not wanting another partner even if one was allowed to come here, no matter how many times I tell him to ask, so one day this township will rely on me for all its eggs.

Not every family has kids to take over their jobs. Milly, whose family makes shoes, is learning to milk Mrs Nguyen's cows. Me and Davy is gonna learn bee-keeping from Mrs Wang next year. I'm looking forward to having honey and wax to barter as well as eggs when I'm older. Everyone likes honey and candles, so I'll be picking up a cake a day from the bakery once we take over the bees. Da has a big credit at the bakery already but he don't like to run it down coz chickens go off lay a few weeks every year and that's when we use our credits with them.

There's nothing I don't know bout chickens and there's nothing the Walter Ticerat School can teach me bout chickens. Luckily school's only four mornings a week or I'd probbly not even show up.

Thing is, Miss Drinkwater don't seem to understand that I'm a chicken farmer first. I look like any kid what's been working before school. And I'm way stronger and faster than any of them. Mind you, there's only twelve school-age kids in this whole township so it's not such a brag. No babies even been approved to be born for five years straight, so it's not gonna change anytime soon.

Miss Drinkwater does this thing where she puts her pointer finger up in the air, her middle finger on one eyelid and her thumb on the other and moves her eyelids back and forth. It sends a message, maybe. If Miss Drinkwater just up and yelled at me, that would be better than this fingers on eyelids rubbing like her brain's in pain and she wishes the government will send a replacement soon.

'Go kindly on this honoured earth, child,' she says like there's no more she has to say on the subject, so we wash our hands, kick off our boots and move inside to maths and then literature. Then we break for morning tea in the playground. Me and Davy share his snack. This time it's two flatbreads wrapped around grated carrot, beetroot, and cabbage in garlic yoghurt dressing, and a half apple and hunk of cheese each. Mmm mmm.

We swallow the flatbreads and cheese down and take our half-apples to play handball for ten minutes until it's time for the next session. The next session is history. It goes like this at our school: maths, literacy, history, art; maths, literacy, history, science; maths, literacy, history, sport. I dunno if Miss Drinkwater is hooked on history or if this is how all the other townships have it, but this is a lot of history!

Yes, I know people in the old days lived in giant

mega-cities smothered in dirty clouds and had lots of technology and lived unsustainably and used fossil fuels and drowned the world in plastics and pollution and parts of the honoured and natural world died and the seas rose and we invaded the wild areas and new diseases took hold and killed most of their children and now we have to stay in our townships and keep our hair short and our hands clean and not make a peep of pollution and not increase our numbers even by one coz we would need to expand our range, and the honoured and natural world needs hundreds of years to recover and rebalance the planet or we won't survive. I'm twelve years old. I've had so many history lessons I know to my core this is how we have to live now. Three hundred and fifty kind, ethical, truthful people on seven hundred hectares or not at all.

I get that. It's fine. We been told over and over we're the generation that waits for the world to recover. We endure the heat. We endure the storms that blow up out of nowhere, giant bacteria-stained clouds that roll and boil green at the edges, the wrecking floods that wash through, the long droughts, the days of smoke as fire burns outside our fences, coz this is what the honoured earth does when she's trying to recover.

We're not the generation who lived easy lives in huge

houses, or travelled the world on aeroplanes, or the generation that died at the hand of strange new diseases and famines. We're the ones who get to live and we live kindly and work hard upon this honoured earth. Our hard work keeps us all fed, even if it's only on our seven hundred hectares with our three hundred and fifty people for the rest of our lives. We endure.

The real history I wanna learn from Miss Drinkwater is what this land was once used for. Why is there a creepy jungle at the back of our township that has extra fencing, strange signs and might have tigers and definitely has someone who tied a ribbon and a posy and a round mirrored thing to a tree?

'Miss Drinkwater?' I ask. 'What used to be where the honoured jungle is now, up the back of our land?'

Miss Drinkwater just looks at me. 'What difference does it make, Shelby?' she asks me. 'Whether it was a city or a barren farm? Whatever it was, it's in recovery and we need to leave it alone.'

I look over at Davy and he looks at me, making his eyes huge. Neither of us ever considered there could once have been a city right on the edge of our farms!

Did it reach to the clouds? Is it dead and black from pollution? Is there ancient treasures waiting to be found?

Gran and Auntie Josie are in the kitchen. Phoenix stands on the stairs tucking himself into the shadows. They're talking about him. He knows by the look on Aunt Josie's face. He's the only one that makes her face scrunch up like that. Like she can't understand one bit of him. To be fair, he can't understand one bit of himself either, so he can't really blame her.

The raven has left a trail of muddy footprints all the way through the hall, down the stairs, into the kitchen and out the back door, and why couldn't the bird just have gone out the window? Phoenix knew the huge thing was too heavy to fly. How on earth is he going to explain this one?

Auntie Josie is scrubbing at the footprints, the *sshshck*-ing of the brush against the tiles scrubbing over her words, scribbling them out from the air. Phoenix catches snippets hissed at Gran between scrubs.

'Sleepwalking again *sshck shhsh, shhhck shhsh, shhhck*
A lock is *sshck shhsh, shhhck shhsh, shhhck*
need *sshck shhsh, shhhck shhsh, shhhck*
wrong with *sshck shhsh, shhhck shhsh, shhhck*
boy? *sshck shhsh, shhhck shhsh shhhck*
I can't *sshck shhsh shhhck shhsh shhhck*
Just *sshck shhsh*
too
sshck shhsh shhhck shhsh shhhck
much.'

Phoenix leans against the cool of the brick wall and watches the mud turn to bubbles. Gran looks up. Auntie Josie stops scrubbing.

'Morning, Phoenix! What's that you've got there?' Gran eyes the sack in Phoenix's hand.

'I can explain,' he starts. 'Well, not really, but—' Phoenix opens the sack and a toad leaps out and plops onto the wet floor.

'Oh my! What on earth?' Gran asks.

'Toads! You've brought toads into the house! Of course you did. Where did you—' Auntie Josie throws her arms in the air and glares at Phoenix.

'It's only *one* toad.' Phoenix mumbles. 'The rest of the stuff is—'

But Gran is already scooping the toad into her hand. 'Well, hello. You aren't perhaps a prince in disguise, are you? Waiting for a kiss?' Gran peers at the toad then kisses its head.

The toad croaks. Even Josie snorts back a laugh.

Then the girls and Walter are galloping down the stairs *like a herd of elephants!* already yelling and talking over the top of each other. Walter's dragging Splinky the Socktopus behind him, and squealing when Frankie steps on a tentacle by mistake.

'Well, carry him properly then, Walter!' Frankie says.

'Did you hear that lightning last night?' Ida says.

'And thunder!' Frankie adds. 'Wolfy was hiding under my bed!'

'Does that mean the drought is over?' Walter asks, rubbing Splinky's squashed tentacle, 'How can it thunder without rain?'

'Was it thunder? I thought it was police helicopters again,' Scarlett says.

'Of course it was thunder! That wind was howling fierce!' Frankie says in her no-arguing-with-me way – and then they all stop and stare.

'Gran, is that a toad?'

'Yes, and she's just been kissing the disgusting thing too,' Josie grumbles and the girls go 'Euuuugh!' and Walter squeals, 'I dreamed about frogs raining and now here is a frog! Did I dreamed him into real, Gran?'

Gran smiles. 'I guess so, Walter!' and Walter beams with his own magic. Gran looks at Phoenix and the girls all turn, taking in the sack and his mud-caked legs, and all at once they scrabble to get a look at what else he's got in the sack.

'Where did you get all that stuff, Phoenix?'

'Did I dreamed all that too?' Walter asks.

'*Why* did you get all that stuff?'

'For goodness sake, it's dripping on the floor, Phoenix!' Auntie Josie says.

'Why would you go collecting a horrible old toad anyway, Phoenix?' Frankie asks.

'Toads are a very important part of the ecosystem,' Scarlett says to Frankie, and turns to the front window. 'Hey, Horizon, tell Frankie why toads aren't horrible,' and the window darkens and pictures and diagrams of toads appear on the glass. *'Frankie. **Horrible** is an adjective meaning unpleasant or bad. Is this the word you wanted to use? **Toads** do taste **horrible**. This is to protect themselves from predators. Some **toads** are fatal if consumed. In some* *cultures, depictions of* **toads** *are of* **horrible,** *evil creatures associated with witchcraft and bad omens, but in others the* **toad's** *transformation from tadpole to maturity is frequently used to symbolise resurrection and rebirth. Other beliefs see the* **toad** *as protector of the earth, and guardian to thresholds ...'* Horizon continues listing toad facts in the Mickey Mouse voice that Walter programmed it to.

'Really, Phoenix, what were you thinking?' Aunt Josie thumps the brush against the floor.

'Ancient Egyptians believed the **toad** *brought children into the world while guiding the souls of the deceased into the world beyond ...'*

'I didn't—' Phoenix starts. He looks at Gran and lowers his voice and his words all tumble-gush out on top of each other. 'I woke up and there was a, there was a, a giant, well, a giant raven. All feathers and sneakers, he had red sneakers and—'

'Old practices involving **toads** *that some people say are* **horrible** *include the dissection of living* **toads** *to remove stones thought to be carried in a* **toad's** *head. Such stones were used as antidotes to poisons and thought to prevent—'*

'Oh for goodness sake! It's not this "troubled child" rubbish again, is it, Phoenix?' Aunt Josie snaps and the girls and Walter all hush and still and Ida swipes the front

31

window to silent. 'We just do not have the money to pay for another round of doctors to investigate your little ... flights of fancy!' Her cheeks have gone red and her lips thin.

Phoenix tries to swallow the ache in his throat and the bubble growing inside his chest.

'Maybe if your mother had thought to have some sort of insurance,' Josie mutters and Gran glares at her. 'Well, I'm sorry. But really! Five children and not a thought for how to provide. My little sister never was one to think ahead, was she?'

No one answers. There's a stillness to the house now. All the burbling tangle of noise, gone.

'Phoenix,' Gran says quietly. 'Did you say sneakers?' Her eyebrows knit together. 'The kind with laces?'

Phoenix looks at the ground and nods.

'I just don't understand.' Gran shakes her head and Phoenix's chest squeezes tighter. 'How on earth would the poor bird tie his laces?' She smiles and it's like she is wrapping Phoenix in a big warm hug. The girls burst into hoots of exaggerated laughter and Frankie splurts loudly, 'A raven in sneakers!' and howls even harder.

'Oh now, Frankie,' Gran says, and she isn't smiling anymore. 'Not everyone is able to see things as they really are, you know. That's why we've to listen to those that can.'

'Oh stop it, would you! It's your fault, Mum!' Josie hisses at Gran. 'You encourage it! It's not healthy. It's not right for a boy his age to be …' She glares at Phoenix, stuck for words, then huffs, 'His teachers say he is forever off with the fairies!'

'I know,' Gran replies. 'Isn't it wonderful?'

Walter comes up and squeezes Phoenix's hand. 'It's okay, Phoenix. I believe you.'

But that just makes Phoenix feel even worse. He doesn't want to believe. *It's not real. It's not real. It's not real.* The toad croaks his disagreement.

'Phoenix,' Walter whispers, scratching at the rash on his arm and wiping his nose on Splinky. 'Did your raven have a white feather?' He tugs at his fringe. 'Right here?'

Phoenix stares at his little brother. 'How did you—'

'Phoenix! Get that toad out of my house this instant!' Josie bellows. 'If it's not gone in thirty seconds, I'll flush it down the toilet myself!'

'Josie! You can't!'

'You can't flush a toad! It'll block the drain!'

And Horizon ripples into light. *'It is prohibited to flush animals, living or dead, into domestic waterways. Animals flushed down waterways can cause extreme—'*

'Enough, Horizon! Rightio, Phoenix, go release Mr Toad over the fence and into the floodplains.' Gran gives Phoenix's shoulder a squeeze. 'He can hop into the stormwater drains and make himself at home.'

Walter tugs again at Phoenix's hand. 'I need to show you someping.' He stops to wipe his nose again.

'Phoenix! The toad!' Josie's face is even redder than before.

Phoenix leans down to Walter. 'As soon as I get back, okay?'

'Hurry!' Walter whispers as Phoenix dodges the mudded prints and kicks open the screen door. He steps outside, then freezes, heart pounding and breath stopped short. *There's a perfectly logical explanation.* But Phoenix can't for the life of him think why thirteen black ravens would happen to choose this very morning to settle on the back fence. They look at him and all at once they start to caw, the noise growing in a demanding, deafening wave. All of them staring right at him with their bright white eyes, as though he's to understand.

'More!' Walter cries, coming up behind Phoenix. 'More little moon eyes! What are they saying, Phoenix? There's one … two … three … four …'

Phoenix's legs tremble and the ravens ruffle their

wings and sharpen their beaks on the fence. Then Gran is at his back, her strong arms wrapping his shoulders, keeping him solid and real. 'Well, would you look at that? I wish I knew what it was they were trying to tell us.'

'It's just a coincidence,' Phoenix says. 'They've probably come for the toad. Right? Ravens probably eat toads. It doesn't matter that they haven't come before because we haven't had a toad before. Right?'

Gran kisses his head. 'Who knows? All we can do is keep our eyes wide to this strange old world, right, Walter? Eyes wide, Phoenix, eyes wide,' she says and goes back inside and Phoenix keeps his eyes open and staring until they blur and burn and he can't stand it any longer. He blinks, and the birds have gone.

Lunch is the main meal of the day, all of our township operating on solar ovens or solar-powered electric ones, coz even woodfire smoke is pollution and we're proud of our near-zero pollution. Although it's been a long time since the government drone's delivered us extra supplies as a prize for our efforts so I'm guessing all the other seven hundreds is just as good.

The drones used to arrive at least twice a month, bringing chocolate, fabrics, medicines and seeds for the doctor to share out and newsletters telling us how great we were doing and how the natural world was healing. Miss Drinkwater would read them out in school and we would all clap and feel good. I miss those newsletters. It's probbly been a year since we had one. Anyway, school gets out at lunchtime and bread gets put on shelves at the bakery just before.

We all race home for the main meal of the day.

Well, me and Davy race down Su Road and then slow to a trudge up Maiava Drive coz it's steep and the sun beats on our backs.

All our roads, and our school even, is named after people who was at the very start of the last great pandemic. I don't remember what all of them did, but it was the beginning of the change that shut down cities and made humans focus on being kind to our planet. Because of that we named our streets and schools after them.

Walter Ticerat for instance, I think he was a man who first discovered the last great pandemic. They say that one was a bird disease. An ancient disease that disappeared and then came back into the world somehow, from where it was hidden under melting ice or something they thought. Like how anthrax came back from old deer carcasses buried in the Arctic. Cept the bird disease was stronger and spread faster, going straight from ancient creatures to people.

I leave Davy at his, and short-cut across the field to my own back door, and splosh water from the rain tank onto my face.

Da, he's not so into main-meal making. Mostly what we have on our solar stove out the back door of the cottage is what Davy ate the day before, or eggs from our chooks

37

frying on a pan. I don't mind. I love eggs and Da cooks them in so much grease they's super-crunchy around the edges and runny in the middle. He cooks old bread in just as much grease so that my lunch is usually bread-chips and eggs. I love to dip bread-chips in egg yolk. And like I said, people don't realise how much food kids need. I mean, up at dawn to fix fences, school, then trudging home up our hill in the heat of the day to eat, then just a little break before cleaning out the barn and collecting eggs, feeding the hens and the chicks, shooing the young roosters up into the old pine tree to fend for themselves so they's not causing trouble with the old roosters, and locking the hens up in the evening. This is hard work.

Da, he's watering and mending and washing eggs and packing and taking them off to the store for credit and trading for grain and food we might need. If I din't do what I do, he'd be working day and night. This really is a job for three people, not two.

'Da,' I say when we're sitting in the shade on the back step eating lunch. 'Do you think you'll ever put in for a new partner?' He misses my ma. I see him talk to her photo sometimes.

'Girl,' he says. 'Do you really want someone else here, ruining the quiet?'

'I guess it'd be okay, if they was nice to me and could help with the work.'

'Well, that's good, coz I already put in a request,' he says, and smiles. 'I got Dr Geraldine to send off my description and compatibility form to the central government to match me up.'

I'm so surprised I drop my plate into the dirt. I'm sitting there with the crunchy bit of bread in my hand I was bout to mop up the last of the yolk with. I point it at him. 'Really?'

'Really. Last year,' he says.

'Why din't you tell me?' I say.

Da laughs. 'I didn't want you to get your hopes up. I mean, we're three hundred and forty-seven and Daisy and Joe have put in for a baby too, and other people are also looking for partners and babies.'

'And mules,' I say. 'And a teacher.'

He shrugs. 'There's probbly better offers than a sunburnt old scruff and an egg farm, coz I haven't heard back.'

'You're not a sunburnt old scruff,' I say.

He musses up my short hair for me. 'I was talking bout you, girl.'

I laugh and bump him with my shoulder. 'You haven't heard anything, or did they say they's looking?' I ask.

39

'See, this is why I didn't mention it. You're getting your hopes up. I haven't heard anything. And Daisy, she says she hasn't heard anything either even though you don't have to convince a baby to come here, just make one.' He shrugs. 'So there's nothing to be done. It's you and me for the foreseeable future, girl.'

I go over to Davy's for apple pie and cream before the earth turns from the last of the light. We sit on the back step and try to figure out what we do bout the posy and rainbow disc we saw. We already decided not to tell anyone else, coz they'd just tell us to stay away, but that don't mean there ain't someone living in the honoured jungle at the back of our holdings. Someone who might have a dog and definitely cut our fence.

'I don't think there's anyone knows what used to be there,' Davy says.

'Then we gotta go figure it out for ourselves,' I say.

'What? Go through the perimeter fence?' Davy asks. 'But that's there for a reason. We can't be out there making trails or scaring wildlife or anything that affects the honoured and natural world, and if it was a city, then won't it be full of poisonous pollution and diseases?'

'Nah, if we go out into the natural world just once.

Just to see what we can see, that's not gonna do much,' I say. 'Just footprints. What if someone is trapped out there by accident with dangerous tigers and whatnot? Wouldn't you wanna make sure they's okay?'

Davy shakes his head. 'Not if there's "dangerous tigers and whatnot",' he says.

I don't understand how there can be dangerous tigers out there, but Davy thinks there is. So I don't have a choice. I say, 'Well, I'm going out. Friday afternoon after chores, when Da thinks I'm swimming in the creek or down in the township. That's when I'm going. You don't have to come.'

Davy nods. He knows me enough to know I'm serious. 'I'll bring a big knife,' he says coz he can't let me do anything dangerous alone. Coz he's a good friend. The best. And to tell the truth, I don't wanna go out into that spooky jungle without him.

41

Phoenix gets back to his room to thirty-four unread messages from Charlie.

– Sorry! I'm back!

– Sorry?! Sorry?! You leave me thinking you've been devoured by some feral beast and all you can say is sorry?!

– No beast. But there was a toad.
And a whole bunch of junk.

Phoenix tips the contents of the sack onto the floor.

– How big is the toad? Is it wearing flippers?
Gloves? Any attire at all?

– Ha ha. Just a normal toad.

– What's the junk then? If you want me to solve this mystery, I need details.

– No mystery. I must have just sleepwalked like Josie reckons, found the sack and dreamt the bird.

Phoenix doesn't look at the burn mark on the carpet.

– I'm just going to chuck it all and forget about it.

- Don't you dare do such a thing! Look. It's
properly boring here. This weirdness is the most
exciting thing in days. Let me have my mystery.
List please!

Phoenix sighs and starts listing. He can never say no
to Charlie.

- Teaspoon, tarnished, slightly bent. Rock, hole in
middle. Teacup, chipped and stained. Old photo of kids
collecting eggs, yellowed and a bit torn. Tarot card,
Wheel of Fortune, creased in quarters.

Frankie pokes her head into the room. 'Hey! Look
who came back!' She steps from behind the door and
jiggles the toad at Phoenix.

'What? I put it in the floodplains! There's no way it
could've hopped back. Where was it?'

'Walking across the cake Josie baked for book club.
There are little toad prints in the icing!'

Phoenix groans. Josie will lose her head over this.
Frankie plonks the toad on Phoenix's freshly cleaned bed
and nudges at the bits and pieces on the floor with her toe.

'Where did you find it all? Some of this stuff looks
really old, Phoenix. It's like it's from a museum!' She picks
up a marble and holds it up to the light.

'Or a rubbish tip,' Phoenix mumbles and goes back to
texting Charlie.

43

- Marble, blue. Postcard – from some city – Eaglais An Phortaigh? Writing on back too faded to read. Knights x 2 – metal. Could be gods? Thor maybe? approx. 6cm tall. Animals x 4 – plastic? But feel and look like rock? Beetle – metal. Letters E S? entwined.

'What are you two up to?' Ida and Scarlett tap on the door, then collapse themselves onto the floor. 'Ooooh, is this the rest of it then?' Ida claps excitedly.

'Is that the toad again?'

'Shhhh! Josie will hear!'

'She's out,' Scarlett says. 'Test driving the new Hydra.'

'Phoenix! Is that a rune stone?' Ida's eyes grow wide gazing at the stone in Phoenix's hand. 'Can I keep it? And here's another!' Phoenix traces the symbol carved into the stone with the very tip of his finger. He slips the stone into his pocket and adds:

- Rune stone (?!) with X. Rune stone with I> sort of thing.

- Seriously? I LOVE rune stones! Photo please! Is that everything?

Phoenix rakes through the pile again, then stops. There, at the very bottom of the pile, is a small, green puzzle piece. It's stained and bunching at the edges. Phoenix knows this piece. He used to love doing puzzles, but he hasn't touched one for years. Not since – and his

44

skin goes clammy remembering the last time he'd seen this piece.

It was the day his mum died. He was home sick and his mum was getting the puzzle down from the top cupboard for him. He heard the chair dragging over, and boxes being rummaged, a thump, and then – dreadful quiet.

'Mum?' he called, but the only answer was Walter's baby-gurgling.

Phoenix found his mum on the kitchen floor, surrounded by bits of puzzle. This piece, this exact piece, was on her chest. He remembers staring at it for ages. There was so much blood, warm and sticky on his fingers, and he tried to scoop it back inside her but it kept coming and coming and coming.

'Phoenix …' His mum's eyes had flickered open, and her fingers reached for his. 'Watch your brother for me, okay? Pinky promise?'

Phoenix held his mum's hand, leaving slippery red smudges on her skin. 'Mum? Mum? You're bleeding.'

'I'm okay, my darling. The angels are coming for me. See? They'll look after me …'

Phoenix looked but there weren't any angels at all. Just a bunch of small, raggedy people with floppy, torn cardboard wings tied on with string, and little toy trumpets in their hands, all lined up with their snotty noses pressed at the windows waiting to get in. That was the first time Phoenix had seen something so strange that he knew it couldn't possibly be there. *They aren't real*, he told himself over and over as the angels banged on the window, louder and louder. *They aren't real*, and he ran around the house locking every window and pulling every curtain closed and when he got back to the kitchen, his mum had just ... just stopped. He shook her and pulled at her arm and kissed her head and thumped her chest, but she didn't wake up.

Walter bursts through Phoenix's remembering, slamming the bedroom door. 'What are you all doing in my room?' He looks tired and grumpy.

'*Our* room,' Phoenix reminds him, and Walter splats onto his bed.

'You okay, Waltie?' Scarlett asks. 'You feel a little hot. Gosh, that rash is really spreading. Did you show Josie?'

'I've beened running. I'm not sick. I'm nevered sick.'

'Why do you think the Spirit Raven brought all this stuff?' Ida whispers, and Frankie scoffs, '*Spirit* raven! There was no raven, Ida. Just Phoenix sleepwalking *again*,' and she rolls her eyes.

'Ravens are messengers, you know,' Ida says airily. 'Birds of prophecy and vision who carry messages through time. All of this could be a message from the spirit realm! Rune stones and tarot cards! Tarot is the mirror to our souls, and the key to inner wisdom …'

'There's no message from the spirit realm, Ides.' Phoenix covers his head with his pillow. 'It's just—'

'Where did you get this?' Scarlett's voice cuts across the others'. She's holding a wooden ring that hangs from a leather string.

'It was just in with the rest of it.' Phoenix shrugs. 'Why?'

Scarlett's stare is sharp. 'It was Mum's. She lost it. I remember her looking everywhere for it. She carved it herself out of a piece of old bog wood.'

'The bog!' Ida yells. 'Of course!'

'I know! I know!' Walter pipes up. 'Mum gived the raven these so we'd go see her because we haven't beened all together—' Walter slaps his hand over his mouth and looks wide-eyed at Frankie. 'I mean,' his eyes dart, 'we haven't beened for ages and ages.'

Frankie glares at him.

'No, listen,' Scarlett's voice is trembling now. 'We weren't living here when she lost this. So how did you find it, Phoenix?'

'Don't be ridiculous,' Frankie says. 'It doesn't mean a thing. We used to come here to see Gran all the time.

It must have just fallen off. I bet this is all stuff Josie had packed up to chuck and Phoenix found it in his sleep. Trust Josie to chuck out this kind of thing.'

Scarlett runs her fingers over the necklace, her eyes bright with unfallen tears.

'But Walter *is* right,' Frankie nudges Scarlett's knee with her foot. 'We haven't been to Mum's tree since Gran did her hip,' and she shares another look with Walter. 'I know! Let's pack a picnic! We'll take the toad too and let him go at the bog so he can't come back again.'

'But Josie doesn't like us around water with Walter when he can't swim,' Ida argues.

'But Mum's remembrering memory-orial seat is there. And her tree,' Walter argues back.

Ida looks at Phoenix and Scarlett. Phoenix shrugs. It's true. They *haven't* been for ages. Gran used to take them every week to visit the place where their mum's ashes were buried. The wildest place around, it was, right in the middle of the old-growth forest. A little urban forest surrounded by hard concrete city, saved because if the river floods in those winter storms, better it fills a bog than streets and houses. They'd planted a tree there for their mum and sprinkled her ashes in with the roots and got a wooden bench made special. Their mum had always loved it down there. She said it made her forget she lived in a city. She used to take them all down there and they'd look for bugs and follow animal tracks and draw and collect seeds for their seed journal – but they haven't been for months and months now. Phoenix doesn't even know where their seed journal is anymore. He hopes Gran knows. She was the one who started it, back when she was a kid, collecting seeds with her gran.

'Come on, then,' Scarlett sighs. 'But we'd better go now before Josie comes back and asks questions.'

Phoenix quickly taps out a reply to Charlie.

- And Mum's old necklace?!

- Huh. A real mystery!
Leave it with me.

Walter grabs hold of Phoenix's arm as the girls scramble off to get ready. 'Phoenix! I have to show you. I think he wants to go back, but we have to sneak him, okay?'

'Who wants to go back? Back where?' Phoenix shrinks, remembering how Walter had wanted to show him something earlier.

'It's a secret so you can't tell.'

'Okay,' Phoenix nods solemnly and hooks his pinkie with Walter's.

'Frankie and me went to see Mum's tree last week. I tolded her we're only supposed to go all of us together but Frankie said she needed to go and no one else was here and she couldn't leave me all on myself.'

Typical Frankie. They had always gone to the bog together. Always.

'And then I finded Larry. I thought he wanted to come home with me, but I don't think he's happy here. And he's not so nice to snuggle. He's kinda lumpy. I think he misses his family. That's why they camed for him this morning.'

'Larry? Who's Larry?'

'Frankie doesn't know I finded him. I hided him in my bag,' Walter whispers loudly.

'But who is Larry?'

'You *know*, Phoenix.' And Walter points to the sack and all the stuff on the floor. '*Larry!*'

Walter flips back the blanket on his bed, and there, lying face down on his pillow, is a very dead raven. 'Larry!'

'Eugh! Walter! You've been sleeping with a stinky old mangy dead raven?'

'He's not mangy! An' he doesn't smell or feel deaded even. He feels like my bears. I like his eyes. They're bright. Like moons.' Walter picks up the bird and gives it a tight cuddle.

Phoenix sniffs. Walter is right. The bird doesn't smell at least. 'Where exactly did you find ... Larry? Was he in the peat?' Phoenix remembers a book he read about bogs preserving things. Something about acids in the peat. There were things pulled from bogs that were thousands of years old and came out looking like new. Bodies even, which people had mistaken for recent murder victims. He'd seen one at the museum last year. It was weird, how alive the body looked. Walter hadn't liked it at all. He'd thought the bog woman was still alive and wanted to get out from the glass 'cage', and he wouldn't listen when they told him she'd been dead a long time. He became terrified someone would grab *him* and put him on display and they hadn't been able to convince him to visit the museum since.

'In the long grass. There was a kinda hole in the hilly bit and Larry was waiting in it.'

'It could be really old, Walter. You should give it to the museum.'

'No! No museums!'

'And it's probably full of lice or mites. That's what your rash is. Lice bites.'

'Nuh uh. He doesn't have mice or lites. See?'

Walter shoves the dead bird into Phoenix's hand. Phoenix pinches it between his fingers, holding it well away from his body. It's weird – the bird is lighter than a normal bird. And leathery. Rubbery almost. Like it's been taxidermied. Maybe Walter found someone's old taxidermy project. Or maybe that's just what bog things feel like.

'And look! Just like you said!' Walter takes the bird and suddenly Phoenix knows exactly what is coming. He doesn't want to see. Walter turns the bird around to stare at Phoenix. And there, right on the top of the raven's head, is a single white feather.

'Girl!'

It's Friday. No school. I don't think the chickens will mind if I let them out late, but Da's still yelling from the kitchen to get me up and moving.

'Girl!'

Being co-owner of an egg farm is all bout early starts, my da says.

'Uh?' I pull the covers over my head.

'Kashvi's lost a sheep. Davy's going up to the fence line, wants to know if you can go too?'

'Yeah!' I say. 'I'll go.'

I throw on my work clothes and hurry into the kitchen. Da's got the fence-repair bag out and a bottle of water. Then he smiles and pulls out an apple like he's the best da in the world. I know he's not the best, but he's my da and he sticks by me and he thought to trade eggs for not just any apple, it's the speckled kind that's my favourite, so I kiss the end of his nose and hug him round the middle. Miss Drinkwater says there used to be hundreds of types of apples, but on our seven hundred we just got three kinds that don't mind the heat. I'd really like to taste hundreds of kinds of apples!

'If I'm not back by lunch, I'll be over at Davy's.' I wonder do I sound like I'm lying, coz I'm at Davy's for lunch so often, why say it? Lying is not kindly. It's not truthful and it's not ethical. Just thinking bout a trip through the fence and already I'm changing.

Da nods. 'Be careful out there. Strange things come out of that honoured jungle.'

'What strange things?' I ask.

'Something big enough to take sheep.'

I shrug. 'But what?'

'Probbly some big ol' dog from way back,' he says. 'Shouldn't bother two of you in daylight hours. But don't go cornering her. Shoo her off back through the fence if she's not gone already.'

I thought it was just a dog too before Davy's talk bout tigers. Wild dogs have a decent fear of people and usually run off when we see them near the perimeter fence. I grab the apple, the bag and water and head out the back door.

Davy's sitting by the composting loo. 'Kind morning, Shel!'

'How long have you been here?' I ask.

Davy shrugs. 'I been sharpening my knife.' He holds up something that looks like what great explorers might use to slash through vines. It's rusty cept for shiny silver scratches along the blade edge.

'Looks useful,' I say even though it looks like the crumbling wood handle will give Davy splinters.

We head up the hill on Davy's property first and work our way along our property as well, until we find my mending wires snipped clean as clean and white wool tufts showing that the dead sheep was dragged through here.

'Who's doing this?' Davy is stunned all over again that someone cut a perimeter fence.

'Do you think,' I say and look at Davy, 'whoever is doing this is doing it to get through themselves or to just let wild animals through?'

'If someone wanted to let wild animals in, why not three or four holes?' Davy says.

'But why cut holes into our seven hundred at all?' I say. 'We're the critters fenced in from the world. Us trapped on our seven hundred hectares. The honoured natural world can come and go and flow around us. No fences out there, nothing but the river to cross. It's like they's free but they wanna break into the zoo!'

Davy shrugs and grins. 'Maybe they just wanna break into our zoo to see our egg-critter?'

I punch Davy in the arm. 'I'm not an egg-critter!' I squeeze through the hole.

'We're really going out?' he asks, his knuckles white where he's clinging to the fence links.

'Yep!' I say and head towards the posy tree. 'Come on, sheep-critter!'

'Even with the tigers?' Davy asks.

'Yep! Da says it's some big dog, not a tiger, and they can have black fur too,' I say confident as I can, coz if Davy takes off now, I don't wanna go on alone! Already the deep shade under these big honoured trees is making my skin cold and the leaves is rustling like there might be something scurrying in the shadows there!

There's a grunt behind me and Davy's through the fence. 'I don't wanna meet some giant dog either,' he says.

We first look at the posy and the ribbon tied to the tree and the spinning mirrored disc-shaped thing. The disc has a hole in the middle and writing on one side. It means nothing to me – *Disc 5 of Series III* and some big swirly word I can't even read, coz I can only make out a T and maybe an O? It's pretty faded writing. Why would anyone need a thing that makes tiny rainbows anyway?

'Look!' Davy says. He pulls a grubby envelope out from the fork of a tree.

My heart does a leap that there's someone out here, in the deep dark honoured jungle who wants to invite us to something. Every envelope I've ever seen has an invitation to a wedding or a birth party or something special. It's bound to be something weird and strange, but we'll get to meet them!

Davy turns it over reading it and I'm reaching for it, but he holds it away. 'It says it's to You.'

My eyebrows just bout hit my hair. 'To me?' Who'd be writing *me* letters?

'Not *you*.' Davy points to the words on the envelope. *To You. 54 Alcott Drive, 3094,* is written in shaky faded handwriting.

'Open it!' I say.

'But it's not to us,' he says.

'I'm a you! You're a you! And there is no Alcott Drive!' I say and pull the envelope from his hand. The corner of the paper tears. It's so old it's turned brown and is falling to bits.

I open it more carefully and pull out a card. A picture of funny birds wearing sunglasses and hats tumbles out as well and I grab it and pass it to Davy. There's scrawly writing on the card. I read it to Davy, *'Hey You, any more ravens in sneakers come visiting?'* This is definitely not an invitation. Miss Drinkwater would have words with this person bout making neater letters.

'Why's it going on bout a raven in sneakers?' Davy asks.

I shrug and keep reading. *'I'm still working on the mystery of all the stuff from his sack. I read that ravens collect things and hide them, but why collect a toad?!* It's like the person thinks a raven in shoes is like a little person,' I say.

'Miss Drinkwater says people was encouraged to believe whatever they wanted before the cities failed,' Davy says. 'She says sometimes it let them pretend everything was okay, but we kind folk have only this honoured earth and the truth.'

'This person who wrote this don't sound like they's pretending. I mean ... a sack? Why wouldn't you pretend it was a little velvet bag or a little basket woven from rolled gold if you was pretending? It's just a little raven.'

'Ca caw!' a bird screams and I jump so high I almost fall over.

Davy laughs like he din't jump just as high. Then he's twisting his head around. 'Maybe that's a raven in shoes,' he says like he thinks this is all a joke. 'It might have a sack of stuff and a toad for you.' He waves the picture he's holding. 'Or hats or sunglasses.'

My heart's thumping but there's no sign of that noisy bird, so I keep reading. *Anyway, I thought you'd like this postcard. I couldn't believe it when I saw it in the shop! Miss you. See you soon, you big baboon!* I turn the postcard over. The front has a picture of a giant bird god carrying a spear, it's a more serious picture than the one Davy's holding but whoever wrote it has scribbled a speech bubble on the front – *Where are my shoes?!* Weird. I slide the postcard and picture back into its envelope.

'How big did ravens used to be to carry a toad and stuff in a sack, anyway?' Davy asks.

'I reckon my chickens would struggle to carry anything, so way bigger than a chicken,' I say.

'Oh. Maybe it's from the dark ages when they used to send birds carrying messages. Maybe they used to send parcels too,' Davy says.

'Like our drones? Maybe the toads were a reward for being kind to the environment! Maybe they was out of chocolate.' I laugh and hold the envelope up. 'This letter looks old but not that old, plus it's got a stamp on it. Remember Miss Drinkwater's stamp collection?' I put it back into the tree. Maybe I'll take it out on the way back and read it again.

'Strange to write a letter to You,' Davy says.

I shrug. 'If a raven in shoes did give this You a toad in a sack, I guess you'd wanna help figure out the mystery. Maybe You is a secret code name?'

We leave the disc thing spinning in the tree next to the flapping ribbon around the posy coz they will help us find our way back, and head further into the dark undergrowth, trying to tread gently. The cloggy smell of damp earth and rotting wood hits the backs of our throats with every breath.

We reach the second fence that Davy talked bout, and sure enough, barbwire on top and signs saying *Keep Out* and a hole cut so big in the fence a whole stack of tigers could walk through. No amount of repair wire could cover that gap.

'Let me go first, I have the knife,' Davy whispers.

'Wild animals never attack front on. They attack from behind,' I whisper back.

Then Davy's looking over his shoulder and twisting round now and then as I push through vines and branches.

We reach the top of the hill and the undergrowth has thinned out but the honoured trees is so tall and thick there's no lookout, so we start down the other side. There's trees and flowers growing in this jungle I've never seen before, all sorts of colours and leaves. Soon we find a path heading down the hillside. An actual path! And what kind of honoured and natural body is big enough and travelling enough to leave a path?

A little way along there's another posy. This one made of leaves and silver foil, tied off with bright wires to an upright rusty metal beam. At the heart of this strange posy is a little leather strap with a tarnished bone-shaped piece of metal on it. On the metal is the word *Wolfy* followed by ten numbers.

I look at Davy and he shrugs. I dunno what scares me more. Wolves or tigers.

We carry on down the trail walking faster now the path is clearer. We're stepping over more rusty metal and sometimes concrete beams or steps or low walls. I'm wondering what kind of buildings was here back in the old times, then I stop dead, coz on the path in front of me is a tiny animal sitting up on its hind legs.

She flicks her head back and forth looking at me with one dark beady eye, then the other. She has a pointy nose and whiskers and don't look the least bit dangerous. Then she drops down on four paws and gallops off down the path.

'Come on!' I say to Davy and chase the little critter. The path opens out to a bare area full of holes, and there's dozens of these pointy-nosed little critters, sitting up on fallen concrete beams, tiny hands held up in front of them, looking around or running, ducking down into holes dug in the honoured soil.

'Wow!' Davy says.

'What is they?' I ask. 'Weasels?' I've never seen any animals like these in our environment books.

'Wow!' Davy says again, looking through a gap behind the critters' clearing. 'Miss Drinkwater was right!'

And in the distance, right across the river, across the valley, a sight that makes my spine tingle. A bunch of towers, all different shapes and heights, concrete and glass, but not sparkly glass, faded, streaky, cracked glass and sometimes a tuft of green on the side.

'It's an old city!'

Phoenix, Walter and the girls are out the back door and over the fence with Wolfy running back and forth between them all before anyone can change their minds. Walter has the dead bird in his backpack, and Phoenix has the toad in the empty sack. He can't stop the buzzing shaking in his legs though, no matter how fast he walks.

I must have seen Walter's bird without realising it. I must have been sleepwalking and saw the bird and found the sack like Frankie said and dreamed the raven and and and – but his thoughts won't stop firing questions at him. What about the puzzle piece? How did that get here? What about the toad? What about what about what about … and all Phoenix can do is tell himself over and over, *it's not real.*

They cut across the floodplains, dry now with no rain funnelling all the grimy street water away from the buildings, and stomp off along the riverbed to avoid the sour smoke coughing out of the plastic-smelting factory.

'Watch your feet with all that rubbish,' Scarlett warns. 'And no exploring the burned-out cars – we've no time.'

Frankie scowls but doesn't argue, and as soon as they hit the forest path, they all race to their mum's tree, everyone slowing at the end to let Walter win except for Frankie, who says it's good for him to lose.

Phoenix wraps himself around the tree. 'Hi, Mum,' he whispers, kicking off his shoes and squirming the soles of his feet into the gritty dirt so he can touch Mum, right there, right next to him like she used to be, all warm and loving. He tips his face to her leaves and listens to the rustle of their mum whispering back, and his thoughts quiet and his body gives up the itch that's been at him lately, as though his skin isn't comfortable on his own bones.

Ida presses her face to the trunk. 'Hello, Mum. A Spirit Raven appeared to Phoenix and told us to come see you. I'm sorry it's been so long.'

'There's no spirit raven,' Frankie says loudly to the branches. 'Phoenix is just daydreaming again.'

'Look, Mum! We brought you a toad!' Walter says and holds the toad up to the tree. The toad blinks and croaks and Walter lowers it gently onto the grass. 'He can be your new friend! Toad, go to Mum.' The toad looks at them all disdainfully, then crawls slowly into the reeds.

'Now remember, Walter,' Scarlett says, 'you're not to go exploring off the path, right? The bog looks like solid ground, and some of it is, but it has soft parts too. Bog holes that could be anywhere off the path. Do you remember, Walter? That green over there isn't grass, it's bog moss. Pretend ground. And if you step on it, a great big hungry bog mouth will open right up, and suck you down into the dark and we won't be able to pull you back out again.'

Walter looks bug-eyed at Scarlett and nods. 'I won't step, Scar. I won't.'

'And no one is to tell Auntie Josie. She'd lose her head if she knew.'

'Phoenix!' Walter whispers. 'I'm putting Larry back.'

Phoenix looks at the girls, all busy setting up the food and shooing Wolfy away from stealing it. 'Okay, Walter, but don't go far. You heard Scarlett.'

'I won't. I'm not silly.'

'And lunch is just about ready.'

'Lunch!' Walter yells and he runs, Splinky trailing from his hands, before remembering that he is trying to sneak. Phoenix watches him crouch down to look at something on the ground and wonders if maybe he should go with him. 'Phoenix!' Walter yells. 'Look what I found! A feather!'

'Great!' Phoenix smiles, watching his brother hold the black feather up to the sun, and twirl it in his fingers. When did they all stop doing things like that?

'There's a rainbow in the feather! Ooh! And more feathers! A whole trail! I'll collect them all, okay?'

'Okay! But don't—'

A crackle of thunder rolls across the sky then, drowning out Phoenix's words. His hair picks up and prickles along his scalp and he looks to the sky. *Like a warning.* Phoenix's chest tightens, and the first small drops of rain begin to fall.

Rain! Actual rain! He can't remember the last time it rained! The girls cheer, their mouths open to catch the drops even though they'll be foul and full of pollution. Phoenix turns back to Walter. 'Look, Waltie! Rain!'

But Walter isn't there. There's just his backpack, dropped on the ground, and his dead raven perched at the edge of the reeds, its moon eyes gazing up at the darkening sky.

We move to the shade to have a drink and cool down after all that climbing through the honoured jungle and just stare.

The city laid out below us is completely fenced off from the natural world like our seven hundred, but that hasn't stopped the natural world from getting in. There's rubble and ruins like what we're standing on for ages, but all overgrown, and then the city buildings standing like a monument in the middle. The plants that have taken over the city is different shades to the honoured bushland all around. It's like a bright patch of greens and reds and yellows and buildings poking up in the middle of all that colour and then round the outside all grey and dull green bushland. Like there was no way to fully remove the city from the land so they just left it to do what it wanted and it was happy to go wild and all jungly. It makes it seem like a magical place where anything could happen. A mass of flowers and greenery, and more strange creatures maybe.

I look at Davy and he looks at me, and coz he's my best friend I know he's thinking we need to talk bout whether we should go closer. But if we start that talk, there's no way we'll be going down there. Going a little way through the perimeter fence is wrong, but this? This is dangerous. We both know for a fact we shouldn't go on down there.

I finish my water bottle. 'You should go back, Davy.'

'*You* should go back.' Davy gives me a cheeky grin, then starts off down the trail towards the city ruins.

'Davy Warusithana!' I say like he's a naughty toddler, and run to catch up.

The path is easy to walk along. It's mostly hard and grey with grass sprouting up through cracks, trees and bushes pushing in from the sides. 'I think this used to be a road,' I say, coz it seems unnaturally straight down the hill, to the river and across a bridge into the city.

'Don't touch the trees on the sides. They could be poisoned with all that stuff what used to come out of those car motors,' Davy says like he's been paying close attention to our history lessons.

'These trees probbly wasn't alive back then,' I say.

'Yeah but maybe the soil is poisoned, so now new trees is poisoned too?'

'Maybe,' I agree. 'I don't even understand when Miss Drinkwater talks bout cars. Imagine rolling along the bumpy ground to get places when they already had the same electric drones we got?'

'They din't at first,' Davy says. 'Then by the time they got them, they already spent so much money on cars and roads and such they din't wanna change, I guess, even though they was poisoning their own lungs.'

'I guess,' I agree.

But it don't take us too long to get down the hill to the river and bridge, and then it's probbly only another half-hour walk into the city. So I dunno why cities had so many cars. It's an easy walk in an hour, even though sweat is beading up on my face and dripping into my eyes and down my back.

I push down through the honoured trees beside the riverbank to refill my water bottle and we sit under the bridge in the shade. There's colourful paint all on the underside, faded and cracked, some of it pictures, some of it bulgy fat words that don't mean anything to us. It's a wide river but not flowing much more than a creek now, making me guess there used to be more water in this river or it had flash floods. Maybe it's our dam slowing the river and sending some of it to our seven hundred instead of down under this bridge like it used to. All the honoured rivers run slower now than they used to. The new trees slow the water leaving the land, and plants that grow in rivers and logs that fall into the water create more pockets and pools for water to stand and soak. This is how the honoured rivers heal. This is how the honoured land heals. This is what we learn in school.

'Water might be poisoned,' Davy says, pointing to my water bottle.

'Don't have a choice,' I say. 'Can't walk in the heat without water, and it's the same water that runs through our township, but if you wanna turn back now—'

'No,' Davy says, his voice echoing weirdly under the bridge, and pushes his drink bottle into the river beside mine. 'Look over there!' he says, and I follow his pointing finger.

A couple of black shells of what looks like cars sit on the opposite bank, with trees and grasses pushing out through the windows and reaching for the light. Cars is bigger than they look in Miss Drinkwater's history books. I thought they only needed to carry a couple of people like drones, so why so big? The cars is all bent and blackened with scabby holes around the bottom and rust colour crawling up and across their bodies.

'Who'd put cars in a river?' I ask, coz everyone knows how important waterways is, don't they?

Davy sighs and shakes his head like his ma does. 'The honoured natural world seems to be trying to get rid of them.'

There's a whistling. Like song whistling, a person whistling, not a bird. And me and Davy duck into the shade of the bridge, shove our backs against the cool concrete legs. The sound bounces off the water, bounces off the concrete. A sound like that, so easy to pinpoint in the open, seems to come from everywhere down here. My body's tense, ready to bolt.

'Where?' Davy whispers.

I shrug and point to the small trees beside the river. Anyone could look over the edge of the bridge and see us here. We should get under the branches.

I check our clothes – pretty dull, a bit grubby, nothing bright to stand out – then I run bent double and dive into the bushes. Davy follows me. Now it seems like the whistling is coming from the top of the bridge, so I creep through the trees and up the bank to the edge of the bridge with Davy right beside me.

The whistling sounds like it's moving away and that gives us courage, so we pop our heads around the edge of the bridge. Davy's breath's hot on my arm.

Right at the other end of the bridge is a man with dark wrinkled skin like he's been out in the sun too much and a white-as-white beard and long hair. His clothes all raggy and his feet is bare.

He's whistling a tune while he's working on something on the other side of the bridge. He's squatting and tying things. This is the person who's been making the strange posies! He has a bag beside him and he's pulling bits and pieces out of the bag and laying them out in shapes in front of him, putting bits back like he's trying to make something perfect. I've seen his other posies and they was pretty messy, so I don't understand what he's doing.

We watch and then he stops whistling, stands up, hauls his bag over his shoulder and walks off towards the city.

'Come on,' I say, and head on across the bridge to see what he's made.

'Wait until he's gone!' Davy whispers.

'He's not turning back.' I keep going.

The thing he's made is more like a sculpture than a posy. It's three bunches of flax tied into a triangle with colourful wire at each point, and in the centre is a brown glass bottle with a single yellow flower stuck in it. Hanging from the neck of the glass bottle is a strip of something shiny and red, which I think might be plastic even though the only time I seen plastic in real life was in Miss Drinkwater's jars of plastic fragments she's collected from fields and streams on our seven hundred. She's got one jar just full of bottle tops in every colour. Imagine that. People just opening their drink bottles and throwing the tops on the ground or in the streams like they din't need them again or care where they went. I'll never understand the past.

On the ground in front of the bottle holding the flower sits a little glass bubble. It's filled with water and there's a tiny house inside with a little sleigh sitting nearby nestled in the white flakes. This is pretty special just to be left out here. I give it a poke and the flakes rise and settle.

Davy nudges the flax with his toe. 'What's all this mean?'

'I dunno,' I say, and pick up the glass bubble. The white flakes swirl all around and some land on the tiny house and little sleigh. 'I think this bubble might be showing us what snow looks like.' I give it to Davy and look down the road after the old guy. 'Let's follow him.'

'What if he catches us? What if there's more like him?' Davy asks, shaking the bubble and watching the white flakes swirl.

I shrug. 'Something bout the look of him makes me think he ain't specting to see anyone out here. He's all head down, chatting to himself, like he's all he got.'

We set off down the weedy road after the man. He shuffles along, stopping now and then to collect a stick or a leaf or pick a flower, mumbling and whistling to himself. He sits to make another posy. We duck behind some bushes in case he looks back and wait for him to move off. Again we dunno what it means when we catch up to where he's tied sticks and leaves with a sprig of foil and a tiny pencil at the centre to a rusty pole. He heads on into the city following the road between towering buildings with giant windows that all look down on us. Most of the windows and doors at the ground level is broken and hanging. Forever open and waiting. Someone has swept glass and rubbish to the sides, and now the weeds and grass have moved into those piles.

'All these bricks!' Davy says. 'And that metal beam, that old metal door. We could reuse all this stuff!' He runs from pile to pile pushing through the weeds like he could spend all day just poking round in the street mess.

'There's probbly even better stuff in the buildings,' I say. 'Come on, we're losing the old guy!'

We follow him deeper into the city where tall buildings throw cool shade on us, and we get dizzy looking up up up the buildings at the sky, at the clouds moving past and us not knowing which is still and which is moving. We stumble and giggle. We've never seen buildings so enormous. We wanna run and explore everything. It's a world of free treasures and amazing sights! But if we lose the old guy we might never figure out why he keeps breaking into our seven hundred.

Finally, he turns right into a wide open street. The street's paved with big slabs of stone and gardens all around, some with vegetables in them. The old guy leans over and hauls out a tuft of green. It's a carrot! He pulls the green off, throws it back on the garden and taps the dirt off the carrot, wipes it on his shirt and just eats it like that. All dirt-flavoured. This must be his vegetable garden. And pecking around in the vegetable patch is two large black hens that look like mine!

'Hey!' I whisper to Davy, and point them out.

'Did you notice any missing?' he asks.

'I don't count them nightly,' I say. 'We look after a lot of them!'

The man has headed up some steps and into a building, so we creep forwards. There's statues, like art statues I've seen in history books, one just a big pile of metal bent up into a twist and another of a woman with one hand pointing up to the air. I feel like she's watching us through those metal pupils and might spin and point her pointing finger at us, as we creep past. It makes my scalp twitch and tingle. There's a fountain pool further into the square, water flat and shiny in the sunlight and making a strange grumble.

'My sheep!' Davy hisses, and points to a pile of meaty red bones near the fountain.

'Oh!' I say. And up against the bloody bones and clumps of white wool there's a lumpy old brown and black rug.

Then the rug moves. It lifts a huge head, swings it our way and lets out a grumbling yawn at us.

I grab Davy's arm. 'And there's your tiger!'

'Walter?' Phoenix jumps to his feet. 'Walter?!' He looks to Scarlett, but Scarlett has frozen, her eyes wide-scared and darting. 'Walter?' Phoenix's voice cracks. 'Where's Walter?' His stomach heaves. And now they are all yelling and calling and spinning circles and Wolfy is barking and the noise gets louder and louder and louder until the whole world is nothing but cold static.

And all around them the bog sits still as death, watching. *Watch over your brother for me, pinky promise …*

'Split up! He could be anywhere!' Scarlett yells, and the four of them scatter, their calls soaking into the bog and ripping away in the wind. Phoenix thinks he hears someone call his name, but he can't tell who it is and it's gone before he can work out where it came from. Phoenix runs to where he last saw Walter, Wolfy yapping at his heels, and he's running and tripping and falling, down the path and under branches, skidding through reeds and mud and jumping over logs. 'Walter? Walter, where are you?'

Drums thump, soft on the wind, and he wonders if there are other people nearby. People who could help. Or maybe, people who took ... Phoenix pushes that thought from his head.

Wolfy stops at a rock, his nose pressed tight. And when he lifts his head to bark, Phoenix sees a scratch of blood on the rock. His breath chokes in his throat. 'Walter?' he calls out, but the word is so soft he can't even hear it over the blowing of the branches.

Wolfy has his nose pressed to the ground now, sniffing in circles, stopping every now and again to cock his head and listen. Phoenix tries not to panic. Tries not to let that gasping fear eat him alive. 'Pinkie promise,' he hears himself moan.

And then Wolfy is off again, and now Phoenix can't even see where they are running with the tears blurring his eyes and his breath coming in hot burning flames in his throat. Wolfy stops and barks.

There, on the ground, is Splinky. Like he'd been dropped and forgotten. But Walter never goes anywhere without Splinky. Never. The sound of drums thrums again, and is gone.

Wolfy is standing at the edge of the bog now, barking high-pitched trembling barks, and for a moment, Phoenix can't see what he is barking at. Just the dark of the bog and ...

Walter. Deep in the bog. Head tipped to the sky, the small ring of his face barely visible above the water. His eyes closed and mouth open and still as anything with the rain falling around him. As though he has been in that bog forever.

'Walter!' Phoenix cries, and his brother's eyes fly open, his head jerks. 'Don't move!'

He tries to tell Walter that the more he moves, the more the bog will suck him down. That he has to stay still. Completely still. But the words are running, spinning circles, breaking apart and tumbling together and all it is doing is making Walter cry. 'I'm coming,' Phoenix says instead, strong and sure, and his brother stills.

Phoenix looks around, for something, anything. But there is nothing except the reeds and the rocks and a log too big and heavy to drag. Walter isn't too far from the edge. Phoenix breaks branches off trees then, like a raft. Or a bridge. *I'll build a bridge to reach my brother. Pinkie promise. Pinkie promise.*

Wolfy has gone now, run back to the others, and Phoenix feels like he did back when his mum died. When it was just him and Walter and no one else. There was a smell in the house that day, of dark rot, funky and raw. And now, here, Phoenix can smell it again.

He looks up at the scraggly angels hanging from the tops of the dead tree, their broken halos caught on the branches and pieces of torn cardboard wing gripped in their hands. 'No.' Phoenix shakes his head. 'You're *not* real.' He picks up a rock and hurls it into the air, and the angels explode from the tree and scatter into the shadows.

'I'm coming,' he tells Walter again. He lies stomach-down on the raft, spreading his weight along the top of the water. *I'll look after you. Pinkie promise.*

Underneath the water, in the very depths of the bog, something begins to stir.

The grumbling tiger pulls himself to his feet and Davy's towing me by my sleeve towards the steps the man went up. But I've been paying attention to historical adventure stories and I know for a fact you don't turn and panic-run from a predator. You gotta face him and creep back all casual, like you ain't afraid and you ain't a threat.

So I'm staring at the tiger, backing up slow, and he's a particularly bony tiger, all shoulderblades and hip bones sticking up in the air, back like a hammock, and though he's stood up and is grumbling at us, he don't seem to be angry or getting ready to eat us. His eyes is blue and milky and his giant lumpy paws is turned in and there's a kink in his tail. A furry pink tongue lolls out one side of his mouth like there's teeth missing there.

He takes a couple of steps towards us and into a strip of sunlight and his bum hits the ground as he flops down and stretches out like we ain't worth worrying bout at all.

'I think he's real old,' I whisper to Davy. He lets up his tugging, and takes a few breaths with his hand on his chest like he needs his heart to slow down before he says something.

'A tiger!' he finally chokes out.

My chickens is still scratching around like seeing a tiger is bout as interesting as seeing a cow. Now chickens ain't smart, but they will take off quick if they see something that might get them, like an eagle. They must know this isn't the kind of tiger that makes sudden lunges at anything. 'Was they real small sheep what got taken from your farm?' I ask.

Davy nods. 'A bony old ram and a sickly lamb.'

I kinda feel sorry for the tiger that he couldn't catch something meatier, but I don't say that to Davy. He's friends with his sheep. 'Let's go see where the old guy went.'

Davy whispers, 'What if there's more tigers? We gotta get out of here!'

'Davy, all we seen is one old guy and one old tiger, but why?'

Davy grabs my arm. 'When it comes to things that might eat me, I don't care why. I only care that I'm not near them.'

'Okay. You head back and I'll meet you at the fence.' I carry on up the steps.

'Shelby!' Davy whispers. But he follows me up the steps into a large foyer like the entrance to the town hall. The floor is shiny white tiles and the walls is giant grey tiles.

In the middle of the foyer is some kind of box made out of large pavers that have been pulled up from the street outside. Carved roughly into one of the large paver slabs on top is the words *Rest now*. And next to the words lies a posy made of a striped bit of cloth tied around some very wobbly sticks, a couple of black feathers and some dried flowers. Also in the posy is a colourful card with a picture of a man on it wearing the same bit of striped cloth around his neck and the words *Security: Perez Stafford*. Lying down behind that is a framed picture.

We lean over to look. The frame is fingermarked and grimy. The picture is of two adults, Perez Stafford in a blue shirt staring at the camera, and a woman in a white coat looking down at a toddler on her lap. The toddler's wearing an oversized T-shirt and is swinging his bare feet.

'Aww,' Davy says. 'She's dressed like Dr Geraldine. Do you think the old guy is that little kid in the picture?'

I shrug. 'Maybe.'

'It could be his parents inside this tomb,' Davy says, and he's right, it's probbly a tomb! He's been paying much more attention in history classes than me!

We look at each other, imagining skeletons right there under the pavers in front of us and take a step back, putting some distance between us and the dead people, still checking for where the old guy might have gone. There's wide glass doors leading off either side of the foyer and stairs heading up on both sides as well. Metal plates showing all manner of names and jobs is attached to the walls. Most have rusting screws so some have dark orange rust streaks and some is hanging, dangling by one rusty screw and some is on the floor propped up neatly against the wall.

Davy picks one up. 'Oh no, we'll never find Raphael Sigmund, Endo something Ologist now!' he says.

I punch him in the arm. 'I think this is the building special disease doctors used.' I point up at the names still on the wall where there's a lot of Vir-ologists in among some Cardi-ologists and Pul-mon-ologists. 'These all look like the names Doc has in her book for consulting if she don't know what's wrong with us. All Ologists. Remember when we both got those coughs that wouldn't go away and Doc made us stay on our farms for a week while she contacted some of these Ologists?'

'And that time I broke my finger in the fence when I was six?' Davy says. 'Doc called an orthopedist who droned out a special little cast and some pills that made it stop hurting right away. I don't see a sign that says orthopedist.'

'Lucky you.' I hold up my little finger that's a bit stiff and doesn't bend how it used to. 'I broke mine last year slamming it in that heavy feed-bin lid and Doc just taped it up with tongue presser sticks! She din't even make the call. She just said she'd been having trouble getting through to them lately.'

'Really?' Davy says. 'Was her phone broken?'

I shrug and wave my hand up at the names on the wall. 'Anyway, that's a bone doctor. I think in the old days disease doctors must've all been in the same building and all the sick people came here to this one building to get well. This is where we should be doing Miss Drinkwater's history lessons.'

'Maybe we shouldn't go in there then?' Davy says. 'What if there's lingering diseases?' He draws the word *lingering* out like we're doomed.

'It's not killed that old guy. Let's just go to the top of the stairs and look,' I say. 'We don't have to touch nothing. I never been in a building this big. I wanna see a bit more.'

So Davy and I creep up the stairs. A raven caws and swoops down the stairs, and we throw ourselves ducking to the handrails. She dips out the door and flies off squawking like we did something to her.

'Maybe she has a nest in here?' Davy says, hanging onto his heart again. I've never seen a raven come right at people before. Maybe she's sick, living here in the disease building. Maybe Davy's right bout lingering germs. So just a quick look then.

The strange thing is, the stairs and the foyer is clean. This place should be covered in dust and dirt for the many many years it's been deserted, specially if birds is nesting in here. It's real old, but it's clean and tidy. The steps is smooth white stone with grey lines running through. Not like the board floors we're used to in the kit-set homes that was droned into our seven hundred. We follow the curving stairway and then we're on the next floor up, clinging to the rail, a large open room ahead of us, both of us ready to turn and run if the old guy is up here.

The floor is white tiles up here too, and there's old and worn white bench seats as if people used to pass through here and sit and wait for something. Most of the seats is in

L-shapes, seat and back all running together, two seats one way, two seats on the other side of the L and in the middle a little flat bit. On the closest lies a posy of pink flowers.

There's a sign on the wall. *Masks are mandatory. Please sanitise, and wait for your number to be called.*

Some of the seats near the outside windows is cracked and crooked. There's outside windows on two sides and I wanna go over there and look out over the city from a second storey, but large dark windows on the other side point to somewhere else, someplace secret and spooky. I need to peek in there first.

There's no sign of the old guy, so I let go of the stair rail and take a few steps into the room.

Davy follows me. He heads to the seats next to the little posy of pink flowers, and tries them out, his boots making a hollow thump on the bottom of the seat. 'Ugh, hard,' he whispers.

I laugh and hurry to the dark window, cup my hands around my eyes to block out the reflecting light, and peer into the room. There's shapes of things in there like rows of giant eggs. Weird. I know eggs. And these is too large to be laid by any bird. Definitely not that grouchy raven. People made these eggs like they made these L-shaped white seats of plastic probbly. But why would people need to make

81

large eggs? White on the bottom, shiny clear on top. Eggs in a dark room. Waiting to hatch?

A light comes on. Bright white light burns my eyes. And while I'm blinking, trying to understand why the dark is now glaring light, I see something else. There's people in the egg things. How? Why? But little faces. Children! There's kids in them. Kids waiting to hatch?

There's some *thing* in the bog. A shape. A large, heavy thickness, moving under Phoenix's raft of branches. His breath comes hard and fast. What sort of beasts lurk in a bog? The water swirls around Walter.

'Phoenix,' Walter whispers.

Phoenix shuffles to the edge of his raft, reaching beneath Walter's arms. 'Slow,' he says, and tries to pull Walter up, but as soon as he does, the raft starts to tip. He stops pulling. If he tips, they'll both be sucked in and under.

'I'm here,' Phoenix says, and he feels the thing in the bog shift. Like the weight of it is sucking the water down, down – and the branches underneath Phoenix spread and the water seeps, cold against his belly, sending an explosion of chills across his skin. The angels clap and cheer and lean forward on their branches to watch, long lines of drool dripping from the corners of their mouths.

Phoenix tries to still. He clenches his eyes shut tight and everything turns quiet, like a knob has been turned down on the world and all the sounds and smells and sights have been muted to nothing more than white noise. And under that hush is ... not something as solid as a voice. More like a thought. *Moon through trees, beat of drums, blue of skin. Listen, listen, listen ...*

'Phoenix? Walter?' The girls are here now, dragged by Wolfy's barks. Frankie's screaming and Scarlett and Ida are yelling at him and yelling at Walter and Phoenix wants to tell them all to stop. To be still. To slow. To *listen ...*

'Don't move, Walter!' Scarlett yells. 'Phoenix has got you. Just stay still.' The girls have the rope that tied the picnic rug and they've dragged a log close and over the edge so it's balanced, with Ida stepping out onto it and Frankie holding it steady and Scarlett is telling Phoenix, 'Here! Take the rope! Get it under his arms!' But he can't hold Walter and reach the rope too, and under him, the thing in the bog is moving, faster and faster, darting, and the angels are screeching and jeering and jumping on their branch now and Walter is shivering and shaking in Phoenix's arms and *it isn't real. Snap out of it! Pay attention!*

'Can you hear that singing songing, Phoenix?' Walter says softly, too softly, his teeth chattering and eyes rolling, and Phoenix tries to reposition himself, to wedge his arms under Walter's. 'It's the girl in the bog,' Walter says. 'The one Granny sang to us ...'

Phoenix remembers the old folk song his Gran used to sing about the girl sacrificed in the bog, and wishes he didn't have such a good memory.

Upon one moonlit night she came, Down hillside steep and rocked. Into the place of inbetween, The Ravened Girl of the bog ... Listen, listen, listen, she sang. And all through the night she spoke, In whispers long forgotten, As the souls around her woke. And in the morn they left her there, Deep down in the dark of the quag. And there she rests, and there she waits, The Ravened Girl of the bog ...

Ravened Girl. Phoenix shakes the song from his head, spreads his legs, steadies the raft, and Wolfy is barking and barking and barking and the thunder cracks again and the bog is tugging and the wind blows louder and the rain thrums stronger and the dark of the bog reaches up, the thing underneath rising ... *Can you hear her as she calls for you? Through time's great swirling fog, Listen, listen, listen ... Sings the Ravened Girl of the bog ...* Phoenix's head is thick and heavy, his vision swims black like the water, and there is so, so, so much noise and the black washes over him and he is slipping, slipping, further and further

91

down into

the

darkness.

Listen. Listen. Listen.

Thunder rolling. Drums beating. Moon. Trees. Moon through trees. Bog waiting, still and silent. Cloaked hoods gathering. Small fingers held quiet in bigger hands...

They wait. Watching for the pitch of the moon. For call of the owl. The hush of darkness. Eyes watching for the first flame to step from the hill.

Voices chanting. Feet stomping. Drums. Drums.

Listen ... They are singing her slowly down the hill now. Step by step now. Their torches licking the dark. Here she comes. Barefooted fumbling. Hands tied, rope taut. She does not cry out with the bite of stones against her skin, or shiver at the iced chill of wind through threaded woollen shroud. She does not struggle when rough hands hold flint to her scalp and slice sharp and clean through hair her mam once combed, untangled, braided and caressed. She leans into those unknowing hands, yearning for one last touch of skin on skin.

They lead her to the edge of the bog. The edge of the living. The edge of the dead. This is the land between. They remove her shroud and she stands in the moonshine, her skin inked blue and glorious.

They sing her louder now. Drums beat faster now. Feet stomp. Stomp. Stomp. Stomp. The edge of the dead. The land between ... listen ... listen ...

Phoenix opens his eyes, his ears, and *stomp stomp* he is back on the edge of the bog, and Walter's safe in his arms, and the girls are rubbing at them both, and squeezing Phoenix's shoulders, and 'How did you do that? How did you pull him out like that without tipping in yourself? Like you were superhuman strong?' and Phoenix can't think of any other time that Frankie has sounded impressed with anything he's done and he doesn't say that he can't remember any of it. Just the bog calling and ... stones against skin. Voices chanting, drums beating.

'You were amazing, Phoenix,' Ida says, and Scarlett agrees, and then the girls are jumping and re-enacting the whole thing in a frenzied loudness that hides how scared they all were.

Phoenix is humming Walter quiet, rocking him like Gran does, back and forth and back and forth on the solid ground, the picnic rug wrapping him tight and warm, and slowly, Walter's shakes are slowing, his teeth stilling.

Phoenix looks to the branch of the dead tree, but the angels have gone, leaving nothing but a ragged piece of cardboard wing caught on a branch to suggest they'd ever been there at all.

Walter tips his head to Phoenix, his thumb half in his mouth and bog-mudded. 'You heard her singing, din't you, Phoenix?'

'It was just Gran's song you're thinking of,' he shushes.

'Nuh uh. There was a girl. And a treasure on a rock. I followed the feathers coz Gran always says I have such good finding eyes and I knowed she'd love feathers and I finded a treasure. It was only one two three steps and I have my gumboots that are made for water. But it wasn't ornerary ground and it sucked me up and...' Walter takes a shuddering breath. 'It's a bird. Made of wood like Mum's necklace. With a stone white eye. Larry *reeeeeally* wanted me to have it. I know he did that's why he left his feathers but I couldn't reached it and the, the rain camed and it's all drownded now and now I'll never ever see it again.' Walter starts crying then, great big tears that leave tracks in the mud on his face. 'And Phoenix? There are more birds in the bog. Thirteen like this morning. I counted all the way up. Lots and lots of moon eyes,' Walter says. 'You just can't see them coz they're all under but when I was sinking, the girl and her birds stayed with me so I didn't feel all alonely. They holded me up and helped us get out of the bog. They've been there *foreverer*.'

He blinks, long and slow, looking out at the still of the bog, and Phoenix goes back to his humming and rocking, humming and rocking, and the rain falling lightly on the ground sounds like words falling in his ears. *Listen*, the rain whispers. *Listen*.

The egg things is ovals topped with glass with rounded ends, full of pale blue fluid. And in them, lying in rows with eyes shut is children our age and younger! Rows and rows of pale children dead in water in eggs!

I suck in a breath and I wanna scream but a man is talking, the old guy is talking. I stand frozen. He's coming into the room but he's not looking at me, he's not talking to me, he's talking to the eggs. I drop to the floor, crouch down below the windowsill. My heart pounds louder than his voice. Thumpa, thumpa, thumpa! Does he think the kids is still alive?

Davy's off the seat and scrambling behind it. He looks back at me with wild round eyes from around the side of the seats. 'Come on,' he mouths, and waves a hand for me to run to the stairs.

I crawl on my hands and feet to Davy, thinking any moment the old guy will yell and come running out of that room. I get to Davy and swallow and try to breathe and my heart is racing, racing, telling me to run down those steps, and past that tiger and up the road all the way back to our seven hundred. My legs is itching to get running but I peek back around the seat.

The old guy is still talking. 'How's your day, Jolie?' he says, and he's checking the egg and moving on to the next, and he has a comment for that kid too. 'Jordan, great day out. You'd have liked how blue the sky was today.'

It's like he thinks they can hear him. *Can* they hear him?

'Kate! I picked you flowers,' he says and pats all his pockets like he expects to find flowers in his pockets, and then he looks around. We duck down and I catch a flash of the pink flowers on the flat bit between the seats right in front of us.

'He's coming for the flowers,' I whisper.

There's a whoosh, a beep, then bare feet plopping across the floor towards us. I scrunch up small, as close to the back of the seats as I can. Davy's a little ball too, one hand wrapped over his mouth and the other across his eyes as if he can't bear to look but his fingers slide apart and he stares one-eyed at me. I put my finger to my lips.

Then the feet pad away and I steal a look around the edge of the seats. The old guy is heading towards a door around the corner. He has a card like the *Security: Perez Stafford* one, on a string around his neck and he pushes it at the door until it beeps and slides open.

'Here they are, Katie!' The old guy lays the posy on the egg capsule. His back is to us and he's bent over examining glowing numbers on one of the egg things.

'Let's go,' I whisper to Davy.

Davy is up and running for the stairs immediately like he's been planning to bolt and I just said, 'Go!' We both tear down the stairs trying to take silent steps, and across the foyer and out into the street, where the tiger opens one eye and grumbles at us. Davy stops dead.

I catch up and grab his hand and pull him away. 'Walk slowly so we don't look like tiger food,' I whisper.

When we're finally out of the street and behind a building Davy takes off running again like his bum is on fire.

'Davy! Wait!' I call but he's not stopping anytime soon. So I run too.

Davy's thudding boots and pumping legs is already off the bridge and up the road before I'm even at the bridge. I don't think I'm gonna be the fastest in school for much longer. I give up and stop to fill my heaving lungs, bent over, hands on knees sucking in big breaths. I step into the shade of a faded cracked building while I get my breath back. It's got a big red *POST* sign over the door.

Miss Drinkwater's talked bout post offices. Your invitations to parties or whatever would go into a box and a person, a post worker or delivery person, I think they were called, would come and get your envelopes and deliver them for you, so you wouldn't have to walk to all the houses and leave them at the front doors. This must be where they used to leave letters for the delivery person.

The old guy has been here. There's a little line of red things marking out a swept path up to the door of the post building. I take a few steps up that path past a cracked red bowl, past a little red ball ripped and flat, then a torn bit of red fabric, a bit of red and white metal, and then a red rock, and a little red ribbon tied around a stick. Sitting on a stack of red bricks is a wooden box with the word *Undeliverable* on the side.

I peek in – there's a few envelopes there all browned and eaten away at the edges. Maybe the old guy thinks someone will come for them. I pick them up. Two of them is addressed *To You. 54 Alcott Drive, 3094*, in the same faded scrawl as the letter near our fence. I look up and down the street, then tuck them into my shirt and turn and run across the bridge after Davy.

There's a hoot in the distance. It comes bouncing up the river to me, stopping me, making me listen. A *Hoot! Hooo!* like a honk of an angry goose but the kind of honk that's not from any animal I know and way bigger, like it came out of a very large machine. Cars is bigger than I thought, maybe everything's bigger. But the old guy was way back behind us in the city, not down the river, so it can't be him making it honk.

Clinging to the top of the bridge railing, I'm hoping to spot the honking mechanical beast. A story to tell Davy, scarier than his old tiger. The river winds between two scoured banks, like it has room to wander from side to side. The edges is crowded with weeds and small saplings, and then it expands out to a large flat valley beyond, the area marked out by much taller trees, old world trees, ancient and honoured trees.

The ghostly honk sounds again, further away this time, well over the ancient trees, so far away that maybe the sound is just bouncing up the openness of the river.

I run on and finally catch up to Davy just as he's squeezing through the fence. He flops on the other side of the gap, panting and gasping. 'Wire that up,' he says, waving his arm at the fence, all bossy in his panicking.

I fall on the ground next to him and pull my fence bag over to me. 'Did you hear the big honking?'

Davy shakes his head, still sucking air in. He ran so fast. 'I heard something far off. I couldn't tell what.'

'It sounded like something huge, from way down the river. Why's there children drowned in the egg things? Where did they come from?' I ask. We've only got twelve kids in our whole seven hundred and none of them is missing.

'He steals them, like he steals my sheep and your chickens, to feed that tiger of his!' Davy says, between sucking in breaths.

'No, he was looking after that building and looking after those eggs. He was talking to the kids in there like they's sleeping.'

'Those is freezers. Those children was frozen,' Davy says. 'I saw ice on their eyebrows.'

'Really?' I ask and sit up. 'They was very pale.'

'We have to seal up this fence and never talk bout this again,' Davy says.

'But Davy, what if those kids need help? Maybe the old guy stole them and froze them or what if he just found them like that and he dunno how to help them?'

'Shelby, *we* dunno how to help them.' Davy waves his arms. 'Ain't no one in this whole seven hundred knows what's going on out there!' Davy grips his forehead like his brain is hurting. 'Don't say anything to anyone. We gotta think on it. We shouldn't tell.'

It's Scarlett who decides they shouldn't tell. Mustn't tell.

'Can you imagine what Auntie Josie would do? She'd never let us go anywhere on our own again. She'd probably never let us come here again either. She's never liked the forest. Says it creeps her out, and this would just settle it. This is our secret. Okay, Phoenix? Waltie? Okay? You're alright now. We don't need to tell.'

Phoenix doesn't want Josie any grumpier with him than she already is. He nods, and Walter nods, his thumb stuck tight in his mouth, the feathers sticking out from his fist like a strange bird. They pile their hands one on top of another's and swear that they won't ever tell, *cross our hearts, hope to die*, and they sneak home around the back and get Walter bathed and his clothes cleaned and no questions are asked. Not even when Walter curls up on Gran's knee and sleeps and sleeps all through the evening and all through dinner and doesn't even wake up for a bedtime cocoa. Gran peers at Phoenix over her glasses. His stomach squirms, but she doesn't say a thing.

The next day is the midsummer street party. Bins block cars from entering the road, and all the families spill from their houses. There's music and food and drinks to share, and Marc Murphy has made a mini golf course especially, and the little ones run from game to game and paint with chalk and all everyone talks about is the rain yesterday and the promise of the drought breaking and Walter shows off his feathers to anyone who will listen.

'I found them,' he says, but when Janey Macdonald from next door asks where, Walter sticks his thumb in his mouth and whispers, 'It's a *cross our heart hope to die stick a needle in our eye* secret. We're not to tell.'

'It's a stupid secret,' Janey says. 'They're only dirty old crow feathers.'

And Walter yells back that they aren't, they're raven feathers and they're magic, and it's not until Gran comes along that they stop their yelling.

'When I was a little girl,' she says, and Janey rolls her eyes, 'we had a song about raven feathers. Now let me see … how did it go …' She holds the feathers up to the light, her eyes flicking back through time, trying to remember, and then she smiles and starts singing. *'One raven's feather is sorrow,'* she sings and hands the first feather to Walter. *'Two feathers found means joy. Three's a message coming, and four a foe destroyed. Five is days of sunshine, and six is for the rains, seven is a loss, and eight is for a gain. Nine feathers found means friendship. Ten is bliss within the home. Eleven is for dreaming, and twelve means you're to roam,'* and they've all stopped to listen now because there is only one feather left in Gran's hand. *'Thirteen feathers ...'* She stops and shakes her head. 'You know, I think the song must have stopped at twelve. They are lovely feathers, Walter. Aren't your finding eyes so clever?' And she hands the last one back and bustles away, shaking the song from her mind.

'Your gran is wrong. It doesn't stop at twelve. I know the thirteen part,' Janey Macdonald says, taking the feather and swirling it in the light. 'My grandma taught it to me coz she was friends with your grandma but her memory is better. She always says your grandma would forget her head if it wasn't glued on.'

'Well?' says Frankie. 'Spit it out then, will you?'

Janey leans close, her voice quivering and she's so excited and full of being the one to know that she can't hardly get her words out. *'Thirteen feathers in the hand, is the one to fear. Because thirteen feathers in the hand means ...'* and Janey waits and waits, then whispers, *'that death is near.'*

Phoenix's neck tingles with the look on Janey's face. Walter looks at Phoenix. Then Janey. And then at his feathers. He snatches his feather back, rubbing his eyes angrily with his knuckle, and walks all wobbly back inside the house and doesn't come out again.

Phoenix types under his covers, his phone switched to silent so he doesn't wake Walter.

> – Charlie? You there?
>
> – I didn't tell you before, coz it was so weird it kinda freaked me out just thinking about it. But when I was getting Walter out of the bog, I had a strange vision or something. It must be to do with the bog gases. Walter reckons he heard strange things when he was in the bog too, so the gas theory makes sense, right?
>
> – Do you think it's poisonous? The gases?
>
> – Charlie?
>
> – Charlie? Are you there?

– This better be good. It's half five in the morning!

> – Ohhhhhh yeah. Sorry. I forgot about the time thing.

– Well? What strange things?

> – I imagined there was a girl in the bog, like from the old folk song.

106

- There IS a girl in the bog! Don't you know?
That song was sung about the girl in OUR bog!
(According to the tourist information office ...) Did
you see her? Did you TOUCH her? You should show
the museum where she is and they can dig her out
and you will be famous! (But maybe cursed too ...)

  – IMAGINED, Charlie! I didn't see or touch anything.
  It was like I passed out or something and dreamed about
  her. But it was like I was her. It was weird. And her family
  were there watching. It was pretty spooky.

- Watching you get Walter?

  – Watching her/me/me as her. They were making her
  go in the bog. It was just like the song.

- Bog sacrifice! People used to do that stuff ALL
the time. Sacrifice their kids to the gods. Unless
she was just annoying and they wanted to get rid
of her. A bog would be a pretty good place to stash
a body. Was it a murder?!

  – Is there a difference? How long do you reckon bog
  gases would stay in my system for? Should I see a
  doctor? I keep remembering it like it's my actual
  memory. Like it's always been my memory but I've only
  just remembered it. You know like when you've forgotten
  something and then there's a smell, or a song or
  something, and you suddenly remember again and can't
  think how you ever forgot in the first place?

– Maybe the bog preserves memories too!
You sucked it in and now it's in your head
FOREVER!

                                    – You're not helping.

– Good. Let me go back to sleep then.

                                    – Goodnight.

– Good morning.

Walter cries out in his sleep. 'Splinky!' he moans, and Phoenix tries to remember if he's seen Splinky since the bog. He tiptoes over to Walter's bed and pulls back the covers, but the socktopus isn't there.

'I'll get him for you, Walter. First thing in the morning,' Phoenix murmurs, and Walter starts shivering. Phoenix climbs into Walter's bed and hums and rocks them both to sleep and his dreams are full of bog water and ravens wearing sneakers and hair sliced sharp from his scalp that falls on the ground like feathers. And then the dream twists and turns and Phoenix is at home, but somehow lost too. And he's looking across at their town and everything is different, the land all skewed, and the only people he sees are strangers who stare and don't come close. There is a kid, hair cut short and scrappy, with fierce eyes that stare straight into his. The kid holds their hands out to him and he takes them, and the world starts to crumble around them and Phoenix knows then that this is the end of the world. The end of everything.

In the morning, Phoenix's eyes are red-hot and itching, and under his shirt is a rash running the length of his stomach and reaching towards his shoulders. 'Bloody dead-bird lice!' he mutters. He should have known not to get into that bed!

Gran calls them for breakfast and Phoenix gives Walter a gentle shake and kisses the top of his head. 'Wakey wakey, rise and shine ...'

But Walter doesn't wake. *Just like Mum ...*

Phoenix's skin turns clammy and cold and he stumbles backwards, swallowing at the great burning lump in his throat that stops him screaming for help. And the thirteen raven feathers fall from Walter's hand.

Me and Davy decide to think on it a few days. I made a promise not to say a thing bout it to anyone, just to think on it quietly the way Davy likes to do.

Me though ... I'm all gnawed up like a mouse trapped inside an apple and it won't take long for this hungry mouse to eat its way out.

Why's there kids frozen in eggs in a derelict city? Was they stolen from seven hundreds like ours? Where's their parents? Is they somewhere missing them?

At home in my room I pull out my two letters to *You*. 'Do you know?' I ask the letters, then I gently open the first envelope and slide the card out. The paper is brittle and thin, like it's been pressed flat for many years. I open it hoping for my answer. This time a photo falls out, of two little kids with their arms wrapped around each other and smiling. The letter says, *Hey P! Look what I found! Mum reckons we were about 6. Check out the front – see that house* on the cliff? That's where we are staying now! Isn't it cool? See ya, wouldn't want to be ya! Hope those toads are leaving you alone.

I turn it over, I hold it up to the light. There's nothing else, but *You* might be P. I sigh, and gently open the next envelope.

Ahh, this one is longer, a proper letter. This one will tell me something for sure.

Hey You. Here's all the info I could find on Bog Bodies and our bog girl from the song. This says they thought the only way they could stop the gods from destroying the world was to sacrifice someone. They think there must have been disease or drought or something world-ending big, but who knows what people thought?

I read until a paragraph that makes my spine tingle.

Are you still dreaming her? It's just like the bit from the song: 'Can you hear her as she calls for you? Through time's great swirling fog, Listen, listen, listen ... Sings the Ravened Girl of the bog.' I think it's pretty great. Like by dreaming her, you're keeping her alive kinda. You know? Even if it is only a dream. It's like she still exists.

I stop and look out my window, like whoever wrote it is somewhere out there. Like they still exist too. Maybe this You, this P, is dreaming the world during the great change, when those who remained was separated and sent to the townships. Where any children born could be raised without fear of disease. Where the honoured wild world and the human world was separated to let nature do her repairing. Where domestic animals and people no longer touched the honoured wild animals or forests, and pollution and expansion stopped.

Miss Drinkwater said it would've felt like the end of the world for the people back then, but really it was the start. The start of saving our honoured planet.

The next bit of the letter is hard to read. Most of the centre is stained brown, like it also once sank in a bog. The words is mostly faded the same shade as the browned paper, and I can't make out the writing no matter how much I hold it up to the window. I give up and skip to the end.

Do you think she likes being in the bog? You always said that was your favourite place in the world. Would you like it, do you reckon? Next to your mum? And hey, do you want to come stay at the end of the holidays? You could catch the train! It would be fun! This person wants to know if someone wants to live in a swamp? With their ma? People in the past sure was complicated. I wonder if there's a swamp around here. How far did letters travel?

Miss Drinkwater said they could travel across the world in just a few weeks. The whole honoured planet!

On Monday, Miss Drinkwater gets to the final lesson of the day just before lunch and it's history again. Such a surprise.

'Miss?' I say. 'Where was all the cities before we became kindly folk?'

'Where *were*,' she corrects me. 'Mostly on the coasts and now, of course, they're all half underwater and abandoned. Now, as I was saying—'

'But was there any smaller cities inland, any cities near here?' I ask.

Davy kicks me in the ankle for my trouble.

'There may have been. I don't know for sure. All our maps show our townships and where they are now, of course, not where things used to be. This is a very ancient land – if we tried to map all the settlements that have been made and abandoned since humans first arrived here it would be a very confusing map. Have you dug up some artefacts?'

Davy glares at me and I shrug back. Then I shrug at Miss Drinkwater. She sighs.

On the way up steep Maiava Drive, Davy's face is red

and I dunno if it's just from the heat and running through town or if he's really that mad at me.

'We agreed to think on it!' he says. Definitely mad at me.

'Well, I dunno bout you, but I already know what I saw and I wanted to think on some other things bout it as well. Miss Drinkwater was a big pile of no help at all. Says she's all bout history, but—'

'You're letting on you know there's a derelict city right beside us – how can you know that unless you went out there? You're gonna get us into trouble,' Davy says.

'We're already in trouble, coz now we know there's frozen kids in them eggs we can't rightly stand by and do nothing, can we? We have to tell someone or we have to find out more ourselves, and how is we gonna find out anything if nobody in this seven hundred knows a single thing bout the city being there even?'

'Let me think on it some more!' says Davy.

He's my best friend in all the world, but sometimes he thinks too much and never gets round to actually doing.

'Okay,' I say. 'I'll come over for dessert and we can talk bout it more.'

'Don't come for dessert. I'll still be thinking.' Davy huffs away with his head scrunched down into his shoulders and his hands in his pockets.

'Davy!' I call. 'At least tell your mas to keep some for me!'

Davy keeps walking.

'I'll eat it for breakfast!' I yell at his back.

Outside our house the doctor is sitting on the step as if waiting for Da.

I hurry up to her. 'Kind afternoon, Dr Geraldine.'

'And kind afternoon to you too, Shelby.' She stands up.

'Da will be down from the sheds for lunch soon,' I say.

'It's you I'm here to talk to, Shelby.' Dr Geraldine smiles. 'I heard you and Davy have had to do a lot of fence-fixing lately.'

My heart drops into my boots.

I nod, scared my voice will squeak and be a giveaway to Dr Geraldine that we been through the fence, we saw the city. I'm scared she can read my unethical, untruthful face. Or Miss Drinkwater somehow got a message to her bout me asking bout cities in class.

'Did you see what's getting through the fence?' she asks.

I nod. If I tell the doctor the honest truth, then I'm breaking my pact with Davy, but Dr Geraldine is also the mayor and I can't lie to the mayor!

'What is it?' she asks.

'It's large, but old and skinny, brown and black fur like a tiger,' I say.

'A tiger, you say?' The doctor laughs.

'Da told me it might be a wild dog,' I start to explain, to lead up to the fact it really was a tiger, trying to figure as I go how to say it's really a tiger without saying where I saw him.

'That's probably what it was,' Dr Geraldine says, not waiting for the rest of my answer.

Maybe she thinks I din't get a good look at it. I nod. If she don't wanna know more, I guess I can be truthful by being quiet?

'Did you get the fence sealed up nice and tight so nothing can push through again?' she asks.

I nod. I wanna say that no amount of fence-fixing is gonna keep out a man who keeps cutting the wire, but then that's a slippery slope to saying I seen a man, and I saw him in the old city outside the perimeter fence. Safest just to keep nodding.

'I want you and Davy to be on the lookout when you're out on the fence line,' she says. 'I've heard that some people are leaving their seven hundreds. If you see anyone don't talk to them, run as fast as you can to tell an adult.'

'I will,' I say, my tongue gone dry at the idea of strange people sneaking in here. 'And I'll tell Davy. Why is people leaving their seven hundreds?'

'I wish I knew, young Shelby. I wish I knew.' The doctor takes her hat off and runs a hand through her hair, making it spike up with sweat. 'Go have your lunch, you must be starving. It's a hefty walk up that hill in the midday sun.'

'It is,' I agree. 'Go kindly,' I say as she heads off back down the hill, leaving me wondering why she doesn't just use her phone to call the government and ask them bout people leaving their seven hundreds and travelling around the honoured natural world like there's no rules.

The doctor waves. I lift my hand to wave back but stop coz tied around her wrist, ends waving free, is a red ribbon.

Has she been to the Post building? Miss Drinkwater has a few items for clipping and tying hair handed down to her, but none of the rest of us do coz we all have short hair, that's how it's been for a hundred years at least. That red ribbon looks just like the one from the collection of red things left by the old guy at the Post building. Has the doctor been out looking for these people that's leaving their seven hundreds? Did she get past the Post building?

If the doctor saw them egg kids, she'd help them for sure. Maybe we should tell her. I'll ask Davy.

'It's the flu,' Auntie Josie tells them. 'The old summer flu, doing the rounds at the moment. Poor little Walter, his body is just fighting it too hard, that's all …' and Gran and Josie take it in turns to sit with him at the hospital. 'They want to keep him in overnight and watch him because he's so little. And has anyone seen Splinky? He's calling for him in his sleep.'

Phoenix takes Wolfy and leaves a note on Scarlett's bed – *Gone to get Splinky* – and runs the whole way to the bog, feeling the burn of hot air in his lungs, and trying to ignore the scratching of his eyes and the itching of his skin under his rash.

He'd tried putting some ItchBeGone cream on it before he left, but that only made the rash sting. The more he looked at it, the less it looked like bites. But maybe the rash was a reaction of some sort? A reaction to dead bird bits, probably. He should show Gran.

Phoenix gets to their mum's tree and retraces his steps, Wolfy running on ahead, chasing smells and snapping at butterflies. And there, kicked under a clump of sweetgrass edging the path, is Splinky, scrunched small and waiting. 'There you are! Come on – Walter needs you, Splinky,' Phoenix crouches down to dust off the socktopus. There is something odd about the patch of ground here – beyond the trodden path and stretching towards the trees, the ground is tufted with grass growing up tall and strong, but here, on the other side of the path, it's darker, smoother and barer, with only a few small green clumps pushing through.

Phoenix lays his palm flat against the ground. *Scarlett is wrong about the bog water*, he thinks. The bog water *has* dropped with the drought. Where he is standing now used to be bog, he is sure of it. He guesses it just happened so gradually that no one properly noticed. But the ground here is carved out, and spongier underfoot. Where he is now would have been a good few metres in from the edge not so long ago.

It's a miracle all of them hadn't fallen through. Bog ground holds caves inside it. Small pockets that just up and give way beneath your feet. What if he falls through now? Phoenix's body tenses and he shuffles his feet forwards, trying to spread his weight.

His phone pings from his pocket.

- P! I've been doing some research into ravens.
Did you know they mourn their dead? And pretend
to hide food when they think they're being
watched, but really hide it somewhere else?
And they use their beaks to point!

Phoenix looks up from his phone. There is a raven settled on the branch of a tree. It looks at him. 'Hello there. Aren't you clever then?'

The raven doesn't reply.

- AND they imitate other animals to get them
to do things for them!

- There is one watching me now.
I'm at the bog ...

- Oh. I'd better not tell you the next bit then.

- Okay. Good. I don't want to know.

- You probably really do though. In Sweden, ravens
are thought to be the souls of murdered people!
Maybe the raven is the bog girl's soul! No.
You're right. You don't want to know.

'Thanks, Charlie,' Phoenix mutters.

There is a warning growl from Wolfy and Phoenix turns. Yellow lights are rising from the bog, dancing above the surface where Walter had fallen in, dipping and darting then disappearing into the sky. Phoenix kneels down and pats the dog to still his shaking. 'S'okay, fella.

120

It's just the bog gases releasing. I knew it was those bog gases giving me weird dreams,' he murmurs, but he can't take his eyes from the lights.

He thinks again of blue skin, hears the drums echo, and imagines for a moment that the marsh lights are messages from the bog girl. 'I don't speak bog,' he whispers, and there is a sudden explosion of lights shooting into the sky, then hanging – as though time paused them right there. Phoenix's skin tingles.

He stands up slowly. 'No way.' The lights are hovering above a rock, submerged just under the surface of the water. And there, on the rock, is the treasure Walter told him about.

Phoenix steps gingerly over the ground, edging closer to the water. It's just like Walter said, a bird carved from wood, black as the bog itself, with ruffled feathers and a bright white eye that catches at the sun. It must have lain there in the bog for hundreds of years, thousands even. If there hadn't been a drought, no one would even know it existed at all. But here it is. Like a gift from their most ancient ancestors. Like something talking to him from before time.

The raven craaaks from the branch and points its beak at the wooden bird. Phoenix thinks of Charlie telling him how the Ravened Girl from the song is somewhere in this actual bog, and before he can shush it away, the thought creeps from his head. *Are you really there?*

If he reaches into the dark water, will his hand touch hers? Will he feel her skin, leather-rough and solid against his own? His chest flutters. Another raven lands on the branch. And then a third. All of them watching. Waiting to see what he does next. *I walk away is what I do next*, but he can't take his eyes from that bog wood bird. There's something else there too – something wedged in the bird's beak… His phone pings again. He knows what Charlie would say. 'Jump from a cliff and grow wings on the way down,' Phoenix mutters and behind him, Wolfy whines.

And suddenly, Phoenix has to get the bird. It's like a tug in his gut. As soon as there is more rain, the bird will vanish again, and it feels too important, too special to lose forever. He knows why Walter cried so hard now. There is something about that bird. It's like it's calling him. Pulling him towards it. Phoenix looks around. Can he balance on the log the girls moved? Can he reach from its edge?

His phone pings again.

- By the way, have you got any of the postcards
I've sent you yet? And here's another interesting
fact I stumbled upon …

'Not now, Charlie ...' Phoenix switches his phone to silent and drops it onto Splinky. Wolfy gives a high, nervous growl. 'S'okay, fella,' Phoenix takes a deep breath.

His phone vibrates again and it's only when he's already out on the log that he hears the long rumble of a missed call, but then the wind picks up and he can't hear anything at all. He doesn't turn back. Charlie can wait.

Phoenix's eyes are only on the wooden bird. His hand stretching, reaching. He is almost there. So close now. Just a little further ...

Another raven settles on the branch to watch.

*O*n Tuesday morning, I'm up before Da even shouts and I've let the chickens run free, cleaned out their water feeders and I'm sitting out the back of Davy's before he's even up. Not coz I like dessert for breakfast. Well not *just* coz I like dessert for breakfast, but coz I dunno what to do if Davy's mad at me. I mean, I know all the other kids at Walter Ticerat Community School and I don't get along with any of them as good as Davy.

Davy's ma sees me sitting there and waves me in. 'Kind morning to you, young Shelby. Are you feeling better?'

'I'm good,' I say, even though I'm a bit sad that Davy might not be talking to me. Specially since I've not told him bout the letters I found or Dr Geraldine's visit with the red ribbon and people leaving other seven hundreds.

'Davy said you had a stomachache last night, but I've saved you some custard pie. Do you want it now?' Davy's ma asks.

I nod. Then I'm sitting up at Davy's table eating custard pie, while he comes down to a bowl of oats.

He frowns at me, then frowns at the uneven breakfasts.

'Kind morning, Davy,' I say.

'Shel.' He slides into a chair opposite.

'Now, don't you be a grouch, Davy Warusithana,' his ma says. 'You had two custard pies last night, and Shelby had none. Eat your oats.'

'Two, huh?' I grin at him.

Davy's ma laughs. 'At least your stomach bug isn't going around.'

Davy turns red, caught in an untruth. We seem to be doing it a lot lately.

'I done all my chores already,' I say. 'You want help with yours before school?'

'Uh,' Davy says.

'Isn't that nice of Shelby to offer?' his ma says.

Davy nods and shovels oats in, like he's digging a hole to plant a tree.

Davy's other ma comes in. Another benefit of having Davy for a good friend is his abundance of folks. One is good at cooking, the other is good at sewing, and both of them is real good at milking sheep and making cheese. All these skills have made me very happy many times.

'Kind morning, Mrs Warusithana,' I say.

'And to you, Shelby Jones,' she says. 'Always good to have friends over for breakfast. Davy, I've just seen a line of sheep coming down from the hill paddock. Can you scoot up there before school and make sure the windmill is still pumping water? It'll be too hot later.'

'Okay.' Davy shoves the last spoon of oats in and stands up.

I grab the last of my pie crust and follow him out the door.

'I can do it alone,' Davy grouches.

I shrug. 'I know.'

He grabs a tool bag off a hook and heads out the back gate.

I follow.

'Then why're you following me?' he says.

'Coz you're my friend and we hang out together. That's what we do.'

Davy walks real fast up the hill and I trail after him.

'The windmill's still turning,' I say as we get close.

'Yeah,' Davy says. 'Anyone can see that. It's just the float in the trough. It's always the float. It gets jammed up and shuts the water off. I don't need your help.'

'But I need yours!' I say. 'I need to know bout them

126

kids frozen over the hill, down in the old city. I need to go back and have a proper look or ask that old guy what's going on.'

'But we're not allowed out there. What if he reports us?'

'Does he look like he's working for the government? He looks like he got left behind when they shut the city down, that's what I think.'

'That's what I think!' Davy copies me, and rolls his eyes. When he's mad at me he can be very annoying. 'What if our township loses its non-pollution status and the government takes away something we've earned? Everyone will be angry at us forever!'

Davy has a point.

I rub the side of my face and try to make my brain take on the truth. 'We ain't got anything for our status for years and if we tell someone, they'll never let us go back and find out what's going on, if they even believe us at all.' I hold out one hand. 'But if we go back and figure it out, we can tell someone exactly what's happening.' I hold out the other hand. The one I want Davy to agree with.

'And we'll get into trouble either way for going out at all!' He waves both his hands at my face and throws them in the air.

I give him a good hard eyeballing to make him calm down, then shrug. 'Maybe not, coz Dr Geraldine came to my place and she had a red ribbon on her arm like one of the ones the old guy left in posies or the Post building. So maybe she's been going out herself to look around. She can't very well blow up at us for doing what she's been doing.'

'Maybe we should tell her?' he says.

'We definitely should do that, definitely soon, but we should know what to tell her first. We'll say we heard a sheep bleating and we went to get her back out of the honoured and natural world. That's a good reason to go out, and then we saw these frozen kids.'

'It's an hour's walk to that freezer place!' he says.

I shrug. 'She was a very fast and very bleaty sheep!'

We look into the shallow bit of water left in the trough. A dead raven is floating in there, up against the float, her sky-blue-ringed eye staring up at us.

The letter's words come back to me. *Can you hear her as she calls for you? Through time's great swirling fog, Listen, listen, listen ... Sings the Ravened Girl of the bog.*

'Eww,' Davy says. 'Grubby thing!' He hates ravens coz they sometimes eat lambs that's born dead. There was a time when the whole world hated ravens, crows, magpies and the like and shot them and netted them, thinking they

128

were spreading the last great pandemic. A sad time for all those birds from the honoured world who din't have the disease at all. It went straight from mummified ancestor bird to humans, missing our birds completely. A great time for locusts and other pests that farmers din't need eating all their crops on top of a pandemic.

'How did she fall in?' I pick the raven out by her legs and hold her upside down like I do to the chickens if I have to carry more than one. Water trickles from her beak, then she shakes her head, flaps and struggles. I squeal and drop her. She stumbles bout and gives me a hard eyeballing for my trouble, then hops a few times, like she's trying out her legs.

Another raven flies down and bounces round her checking her out, then she caws and they both fly off over the hill towards the city. I swear the wet one is looking back at me.

'Is you coming?' I whisper, as if that's what the raven's asking. Is she calling me through time's great swirling fog? I'm trying to listen, listen, like the letter said.

Davy shakes his head. 'I'm not going. It's too dangerous.' Water gushes into the trough.

I sigh, trying to forget bout the creepy raven. 'Okay.' I turn and head back down the hill.

'What do you mean, okay?' Davy shouts after me.

'Okay!' I say, jogging in great downhill strides. 'You don't have to go back out!'

'But don't you go back out either!' he shouts.

'I won't!' I say without turning around, and whisper, 'You're not the boss of me, Davy Warusithana.'

'Don't you lie to me, Shelby Jones!'

I just wave. 'See you, wouldn't wanna be you!'

'What does that mean?' Davy yells. 'That's just weird!'

Phoenix trembles on the log. His fingers stretch – just a little further, and ... The whole world has turned quiet and still. The wind has dropped and even Wolfy has stopped barking. The marsh lights are still floating up, rising around Phoenix, bubbles of gas caressing his cheek. He lifts his gaze –

and he sees her. Hovering at the very edge of his vision, the girl from the bog, barefooted and blue skin shining, risen up among the lights.

She is talking to him – not in words, but in silver clouds that wisp from her mouth and hang in the air. Her hand flutters, reaching for him, and he feels her fingers press the skin on his shoulder, cool and firm. As real and strong and sure as Gran's arms wrapping him tight – and suddenly the bog is rising around them, the sun twisting to the black of night, all the heat gone from the world, and Phoenix is no longer Phoenix, he is no longer lying on the log, but standing, bare feet edging the water, blue-fleshed, his tongue pushing strange words through strange teeth and he is watching through widened eyes, he is –

remembering…

She looks, eyes wide, at the rope that is not for weaving. The sharpened sticks that are not for trapping. The heavy stone that is not for grinding. The blade that is not for skinning…

And now she is scared. She searches the huddled, hooded mass for her mother, her father. But those eyes that once loved and delighted will not find her again. Those ears will not turn to her call, her keen, her feared cry.

Now the ropes tighten and sticks twist and steady. Her hands are released and cupped around the carved offering, just as her feet are bound and tied to the stone – 'stone from our caves so she may step …' – and the woven hazel collar is tightened around her neck – 'wood from our hills so she may hear …' She is hushed by the collar's tugging and biting, by the air thin in her lungs, by the drink, foul and bitter, poured on her tongue, in her mouth, down her throat – 'drink enough so she may speak …' – and she is stilled into calm by the nips of the blade against her arms – 'blood enough so she may see …'

'Mam,' she whispers, but the sound does not leave her lips.

132

They unwrap the ancient skull from its leathered pouch. She does not look into those empty eye holes. She does not want to imagine all she will see when she looks through them. They tighten the skull around her head, twist by slow twist, their voices rising higher, their hum louder in their throats. The skull holds her still in its knowing, and she is glad of the shaved hair now, her bare skin better to feel the sureness of those ancient bones.

She is entering the bog. 'This we offer. This we choose to do.' Sticks stake and stone holds. The bog skin is becoming her skin, the heavy-earthed water cool against the burning tight of the rope. The cold bog blood surges and flows in her, around her as her own seeps and blends. Voices are whispering in her ears now, on her tongue now, filling the night sky with warbled callings and seeings, with the knowings and tellings of those gone before. The stick twisting the collar tight around her neck loosens, just enough to keep the veil between the worlds open for a little more ...

She is no longer the child who giggled and played, the daughter who kissed, the sister who sang and cuddled, the friend who whispered secrets and planned futures. She is the messenger of the living and the speaker for the dead. Listen ...

And they do.

All

through

the

night.

Slowly, slowly. The sky above is lightening. She watches the stars disappear, one by one, the seeds of their light falling in droplets of rain that hang from the branches.

The words on her tongue tremble and fade. The voices in her ears turn to nothing but the last slow beatings of her heart. Thunder cracks the skies apart in welcome. She feels the first drop, cool on her face, and smiles. It is working. It is already working.

She reaches a hand to the Message Rock. Feels the bumps rising up under her fingertips, the energy of the ancient rock words moving slow through her skin. She imagines the messenger from the beginning of the earth, imagines the stone carving stone, the marks to whisper through time, and she remembers then the offering held tight in her own fist. She touches the wooden bird to her lips, and places it gently on the rock.

The ravens watching from the trees spread their wings and take to the skies, their calls echoing her ears. She watches them falter, and fall, feather-fast and heavy as stones around her slowly sinking body, called down by the offering to soul guide through the ever-open mists. She feels their thuds. Touches their wings that will no longer fly in earthen skies. She finds their eyes, gives her ears to their last breaths.

Here she will stay. No longer quite a child, and not yet quite an adult, in the place between this world and the next.

Here she will stay. Not quite dead, they say, and never again quite living.

Can you hear her call the ravens? Can you?

Listen, listen, listen …

Phoenix's eyes open. He is back on the bank, Wolfy licking at his face and pawing at his chest. And in his hand is the carved raven – *the offering* – and for a moment, the wood ruffles beneath his touch.

He sees then how his skin is cracked with mud, all along his arms and legs and face and hair, covering his body, and his fingers find the red, raw rope burn still pulsing on his neck. As though it really was him who was led into that bog just now. Him who felt the collar tighten, the skull heavy on his own head. And for the first time ever, Phoenix doesn't try to make logical sense of it. Maybe Gran's right. Maybe it is a gift after all.

All around him on the ground are marks, etched deep into the bank. The same few markings, drawn over and over again. Phoenix knows what they are. He can feel the shape of them under his fingers still. These are the carvings from the Message Rock. *Stone grating stone, the marks to whisper through time.*

Phoenix rubs at the raw skin on his neck and looks more closely at the carved raven. There is so much detail – each talon, each feather, it all looks so real. Phoenix peers at the thing wedged in the bird's beak – it's a seed. Big and black with a whorl in the middle like a finger-print, and speckled with the most magnificent red he's ever seen. Phoenix wonders if the bog made the speckles that colour, or if it is the colour the seed normally is. He tries to remember if there's anything this colour in their seed journal, but he knows he has never seen one like this before. It looks more like a jewel than a seed.

Phoenix wriggles at the seed like a loose tooth, and it falls from the bird's beak into his palm. Phoenix knows then what he has to do. He grabs his phone and Splinky and runs back along the path to his mum's tree, legs buzzing and shaking and stumbling. The rain is falling harder now, and Phoenix uses his fingers to pull at the earth, the dirt pushing at his nails. Wolfy wags his tail and joins in, barking at this new game. And when the hole is big enough, Phoenix raises the seed to his lips, just as the offering was raised to the lips of the bog girl, and he plants the seed carefully in the hole. 'Watch over it, Mum.'

The droplets of rain hang from the branches of his mum's tree like the seeds of stars, and without pausing, Phoenix takes a stone and carves deep into the bark on her trunk. There's a push against his hand of another smaller hand, guiding his, getting the shapes just right; there's the gentle rumble inside his chest that fills his body with warm, and the wordless whisper running through his mind.

The shadows around the tree thicken and twist, and the shape of the Ravened Girl fades into the leaves. Phoenix runs his fingers over the carving, and even though he doesn't know what they mean, these shapes, these runes, they are important, and they are here now, out in the world, in *his* world. Like a message through time.

I'm super nice to Davy for the next two days at school. Not mentioning the city like he wants and it's funny coz that just makes him suspicious, like he's the one who wants to talk more on it now but he can't bring himself to start off. And that's a shame, coz I'm dying to show him the strange letters!

In history, I ask Miss Drinkwater if there's any swamps near our seven hundred. Davy's glaring at me like I'm bout to get us into trouble.

'Yes, Shelby,' she says. 'When I was a child there were a lot of mosquitos after every storm and we had to watch for mosquito diseases, but now there are fewer storms and more insects that eat mosquitos, so it's not such a problem. You remember I told you how after they poisoned the birds, mistakenly thinking they were spreading the last great pandemic, there were too many insects, so they poisoned the insects? This included all the honoured insects that eat mosquitos. It took a long time to rebalance.'

'Was it a big swamp?' I ask.

'Swamps are a vital part of our honoured ecosystem. They collect run-off water from hills and give the pollution time to sit, be converted by plants and bacteria, or offer room for rivers to spread in flood times, so possibly it was growing and shrinking all the time. Now with all the hillsides regrown and the worst of the storm years behind us, it might be smaller.'

There's a knock on the door, and the doctor is standing there.

'Come in, come in, kind welcome to you, Dr Geraldine,' Miss Drinkwater says.

I look at Davy and he looks at me, like we're bout to be told off in front of the whole class for going through the fence. Davy's shrinking in his chair and sliding under his desk like he'll vanish completely in a minute.

'I just wanted to come and tell you all the outcome of our township meeting,' the doctor says.

'Please,' Miss Drinkwater says.

Dr Geraldine heads to the front of the class. 'School, you may not have heard but it's come to our attention that people from the other seven hundred townships are now going through their perimeter fences and accessing the land around their townships.'

Everyone gasps like it's the worst news ever. Some kids is saying, 'Why?' and the doctor looks at me and Davy like we already know, and though I said I'd tell Davy, I really haven't coz what if that makes it even more unlikely for him to come back out with me?

My scalp burns with the untruth of promising the doctor and then letting her down. I know full well staying silent is same as lying. But those frozen kids! Someone needs to find out what happened to them.

'I'm unsure why they're doing this,' the doctor says. 'My phone has been cut off for a while so I can't communicate with our neighbours or the central government. Mr Hajji has seen a stranger by our dam.'

The word *stranger* sends a shock of terror around the class, and there's gasps and then whispers.

The doctor holds up her hands. 'Don't worry. What we'll do is have two adults patrolling day and night. If you see any strangers, I understand you might be alarmed. We're all kind folk on this honoured land. We've all been living sympathetically with our environment and I'm not suggesting that anyone coming here might have bad intentions, but I still want you to not talk to them or go anywhere near them at all and run real fast to find an adult. You all look like very quick children.'

There's big chatter from the other kids bout how fast they'll run from the scary people and who's the fastest and a couple turn to me. 'Uh ah,' I say. 'Davy beat me the other day. Acted like a tiger was after him.'

Davy kicks me under the desk. Gives me a stink-eye scowl.

'Why was you talking bout tigers and asking bout swamps, Shelby Jones?' Davy asks me on the way home for lunch.

I shrug. 'I just have a big interest in our honoured natural world.'

'You're up to something,' Davy says. 'Does our river lead to a swamp?'

'Probbly, but we'll never know, coz we're never going through the fence again.' I shrug.

'And now there's more people out there, not just some old guy, we're definitely not going through the fence again,' he says.

'Absolutely, Davy Warusithana. You's one hundred per cent correct.'

I leave Davy standing on the road behind me with his

arms crossed, stubbornly staring at me through squinty eyes. 'We's truthful people, Shelby Jones!' he yells.

Friday morning I get up early and let the hens out and head straight up the back of our holding. I check for the two adults who's supposed to be patrolling and don't see them, so I unwind my mending wires and let myself through the fence.

After wedging the letters to You in the crook of the tree with the first one, I head off up the trail under the tall dark trees. I tread soft as I can so that I'll be the one sneaking up on anything instead of the other way around. Birds tweeting, chirping and warbling fills the jungle. So much louder and so many more birds than I ever heard on the open land of our seven hundred. Sometimes I see a shape flitting away overhead through the branches, but mostly it's just birdsong.

There's one that sounds like it's trying to imitate Da hammering a metal post into the ground to make a fence to keep chickens off the new grass. Makes me wonder if these birds know more bout us than we know bout them. Then one bird yells, '*Ca ca caaaaoooooow!*' in a deep raveny old-man-groaning way and all the other birds stop for a moment, like they's thinking bout what the raven just said.

I stop too. I stop dead in the silence, in the cool shade of the dark jungly trees, and think bout going back. From a long way away comes a faint '*Ca caaaaoooow*'. And all the birds start up again. Maybe they's talking bout the ravens. Maybe they's talking bout me. I turn around to head back, but it feels so wrong to give up, to go home. Right down in the base of my skull I have a nagging that someone needs my help and I gotta be brave.

I find my way down the trail to the holes of the little critters. From looking in the books at school, I think they's meerkats. Meerkats is not natural. I reckon there might have been a zoo around here somewhere and the tiger and the meerkats is the descendants left over from that.

The critters chitter and scamper away and a few sit up looking like they might be ambushed on all sides. 'Just me,' I say as I pass on through and head down to the old road. A raven sits in the centre of the road and takes off before I get close. If she's the raven I fished from the trough she could be a bit friendlier than that!

I stop and listen hard coz the letter said a girl was calling the ravens. But I can't hear her calling this one. These letters is like a window to a whole other world. One where I can't understand anything the way I understand my life on our seven hundred. But I wish I did understand the letters. A girl sunk in a bog who talks to ravens. How strange.

It's cooler than last time so I'm travelling faster and it's odd to know where I'm going, like I belong here as much as that old guy. I don't even hide when I see him heading away up a side street, climbing through the body of an old vehicle that might've been a bus and is now a rusty shell, looking like it's been put there like a barrier to entering the street. It's got blackened walls, like it got burnt, and on the black windows that's still in the frames, there's writing that's cracked and peeling, words like *NO!* and *SAVE OUR CITIES*. In front of the bus is chunks of bricks like from smashed-down walls, so now the only way past is through the bus.

I dunno how life ended in this city, but maybe it wasn't as simple as Miss Drinkwater says. Maybe people was barricaded in or out of some parts of it at the end. Maybe they had to be taken to the townships angry and arguing, not understanding why they had to leave. Strange to think that even with pollution and disease all around them, they would complain bout heading out to a nice safe seven hundred. Complain bout being saved.

Miss Drinkwater likes to say that the past is a foreign land. Every time she says it I ask her what it means. And those times she don't rub her eyelids back and forth and breathe out my name like I've kicked her in the shin. She says, 'It means we don't have the background knowledge to fully understand the past because we only know how things are now.'

I reckon that's what the history of this derelict city is to me. Something I'll never get to understanding coz I don't have background knowledge bout what people were like back then. I only know kind folk who live simple lives.

The tall buildings block the sun, hem me in like I could be trapped at any moment. I prefer the cool creepy jungle and nattering birds to this. The old buildings creak and scratch and their big windows stare darkly at me as I pass. I'm not surrounded by treasures and things to explore today, not when I'm alone. Sometimes my reflection moves in a grimy windowfront at street level and I stop and stare, make sure the thing moving is just me!

The old guy's strange posies is everywhere and I guess they must make him feel safe. All these little things tied to poles and doorhandles, showing he's been there. Is that why he does it?

I carry straight on to the virus doctors' building in the square. My two chickens is scratching bout in the garden eating his silverbeet, but the tiger's not around. I grab the card marked *Security: Perez Stafford* from the tomb in the entry hall and run up the stairs.

My heart's knocking on my ribs by the time I get to the top and I dunno if it's from running up stairs or that I'm scared. I gotta admit, I'm terrified without Davy here. One more visit, that was all I asked. Just to understand. Adventures ain't adventures when you're alone. When you're alone they's just scary things you have to live through so you can tell someone later. If you survive!

I take the card and wave it all around the door to the darkened room like I saw the old guy do. A little panel beeps. The door slides open with a whoosh, and it's a little entry porch with another set of doors ahead of me. The doors behind me close and I'm in a room just big enough for one. The lights come on and my heart leaps again. It's not too late to turn around and run home, if I can get the doors behind me open again. But I'm so close, and the old guy is away. I gotta go in and find out more.

Then air hits me on all sides, blasting me like it wants me gone and I suck in a breath to scream but the door ahead slides open and I'm in. Gasping and hanging on to the wall to slow my heart. The air in here is different too. It's all iced cold. How can the old guy stand it?

I go to the first egg. A faded posy of flowers sits on top. It's the girl the old guy called Katie. She's lying there sealed under see-through plastic, in a pale blue liquid, head bald, blue lines drawn on her skull, eyebrows and eyelashes a little white at the ends like they's got a touch of frost, just like Davy said. She's wearing a pale blue shirt and shorts and there's tubes and wires under that blue shirt, and tubes snaking up to her nose. They wouldn't do that to someone who was truly dead. The name *Katherine Jun Su* is written on a plaque on the end of the pod.

But Su Road is where the bakery is. Is this the original girl the road got named after? The plaque says *Born 26 April 2018*, so it must be. I'm gonna be asking Miss Drinkwater a few questions bout street names when I get back to school.

Underneath the plaque there's a screen and a glass case. In the glass case is a picture of Kate with her family maybe. Ma, Da, and a little white toy cat. The real toy cat sits under the glass too, and a medal on a faded blue ribbon that says *Art Prize 2027*, along with a picture of a garden made entirely of strips of bright orange, lime and pink flowery fabric. It's good art. Amazing fabric. Better than our weavers make. I can see why she got a prize for it.

There's two buttons on top of the case. One says *Pre-recorded* and the other says *Interactive*. I hit *Pre-recorded* and the dark square of glass lights up. I jump back. Music plays. It's too loud! It bounces off the hard floors and walls and glass, echoey. I back away. I gotta get out of here!

But no one comes running. Instead Kate appears on the square of glass, alive, with lots of hair, and not frozen. She smiles right at me!

Phoenix's phone vibrates again in his pocket, and he wakes. It's almost dark now. He can't believe he fell asleep, curled up like a toddler against his mum's tree. A wave of panic starts in his gut, thinking how the girls would all be worrying about where he is and what's happened to him. He looks down at his phone. *18 missed calls. 10 new messages. 3 new alerts.* Only one of those messages is from Charlie. His breath catches in his throat. *Walter.* Has something happened to Walter?

Phoenix jumps to his feet, Splinky and the carved bird held tight against his chest, and he scrabbles through the messages, trying to walk and read and listen all at once.

'Phoenix! Come back! You have to come back! Quickly! We've been ... just ... come home!' That was Scarlett, and it sounded like she was crying, but then they'd all phoned, all the girls, all sounding just as strange.

And then Phoenix sees the notification flashed across his screen.

THIS IS A CRIMSON ALERT FOR ANYONE LIVING IN ZONES 87, 88, 89 AND 90. A STATE OF EMERGENCY HAS BEEN DECLARED. RETURN TO YOUR HOMES IMMEDIATELY. FROM 3PM TODAY, ANYONE DISCOVERED OUTSIDE THEIR PRIMARY PLACE OF RESIDENCE WILL BE DETAINED FOR TESTING AND QUARANTINE.

Phoenix checks the time – 5.13 pm. Overhead, a helicopter splits the quiet into pieces, the light from its search beam gliding over the tops of the trees.

Phoenix darts behind a tree, holding Wolfy tight to his chest, his heart matching the banging thrum of the helicopter blades. *Detained for testing and quarantine … detained …* As soon as the helicopter has circled back around, Phoenix runs. Back up the forest path, along the river, past the burnt-out car, keeping to the thick dark shadows of the trees. He stops when he gets to the main road, crouching low behind a bush, Wolfy calm and quiet at his heels, as though he knows they are hiding.

There are patrols out already. Security and police with their suits and shields and face masks, looking more like beekeepers than police. Beekeepers, with large batons and guns and dogs and radios that buzz in their hands and torches to search for anyone out after curfew. They are at the end of the street, their torches sweeping back and forth, dipping into every shadow, behind every bin, every car. Every bush. They are walking slowly, methodically towards Phoenix.

A police van rumbles past. The windows are tinted, a small hand pressed pale and tight against the glass. Smaller than Phoenix's hand. His teeth begin to chatter.

The patrol is getting closer. It will only be a few minutes more and—

One of the dogs raises its head, looks right at Phoenix and barks. Phoenix doesn't think – he leaves the bush, diving behind a parked car and scraping all the skin from his palms. The torch beams flash along the edge of the trees. The dog keeps barking and now its handler is letting it tow them towards Phoenix.

His phone rumbles in his pocket, the vibration alarm-loud in Phoenix's ears. He's trapped. If he runs, they'll see him and run him down and throw him in the van. If he stays, they'll find him and throw him in the van. His chest tightens. A sob chokes in his throat.

And then, Wolfy runs. Straight out from behind the

car, barking and growling and running loops around the search dog, snapping at its legs and the dog is trying to ignore him, trying to bark and get to Phoenix, but Wolfy won't let up. And he's nipping at the handler now, pulling at their pant legs, growling in his little-dog growl and the handler is kicking out and trying to get him to *let go!*

Phoenix doesn't wait for a second chance. He takes off, crouched low and sprinting behind the line of parked cars as the lights in the houses turn on and the people watch from behind their windows. The handler yells. Wolfy yelps. And this time the sob comes out, loud and scared.

Phoenix keeps running.

'Oh thank goodness!' Ida grabs Phoenix and hugs him tight. 'We were so worried. And the police are out looking for people, and Gran and—'

'Where were you?' Scarlett has grabbed him now. 'Why are you covered in mud?'

Phoenix squirms away and drops down to hug Wolfy, who's come limping through the fence after him. He breathes in his brave-dog smell and Wolfy gives him a lick and wags his tail.

'Didn't you see our calls?'

'What happened to your neck? Did someone hurt you?!'

A drone whines overhead, and Wolfy barks, growling and howling at the flashing lights.

'Shush!' Scarlett says then. 'Come inside, quickly now. Listen, Phoenix. We've been locked down. The orders came through hours ago. It's lucky you weren't caught.' She's trying not to sound worried, but her voice shakes and she turns from him so he doesn't see the scared in her eyes. 'It's not the summer flu. And it wasn't just Walter who's sick. Six others turned up at the hospital. All with fevers and all of them kids from our midsummer street party. And there are reports of another three kids just now too. They don't know what's causing it, but ...' There is something Scarlett isn't telling him. She takes a deep breath.

'Auntie Josie and Gran, they were both at the hospital with Walter when the State of Emergency was declared. It went into lockdown immediately. They won't let anyone leave. And then, when Janey Macdonald ...' Scarlett swallows. 'She *died*, Phoenix. Early this morning. Just like that.' Scarlett looks at Phoenix and they are both remembering the look on Janey's face – *thirteen feathers in the hand is the one to fear ...*

But it doesn't make sense. How can someone just, just not be there anymore? She was right there. Just yesterday. They all saw her and spoke to her and, and, and. Just like that?

'She died,' Scarlett says again, like she can't get her head around it either, 'and then there was the crimson alert blaring out all over town, and within the hour the army was called in and the fences went up around our zones and no one can leave. And no one can come in.'

Phoenix remembers the fences and the lockdown from before. From when the pandemic crept across the world. He remembers how at first no one really believed it would spread as fast as it did. No one believed it could. And then how quickly everything stopped and changed.

He was scared of the fences the last time, at how high they were and how sharp the razor wire was on top. He was scared by the police and army that marched up and down in their white beekeeper germ protection suits and masks and guns, and the drones that would shine through the windows to make sure people were obeying the rules, but Gran had said they were protecting them, that was all, just like in the old days. Stopping the virus spreading, and Phoenix had imagined a great big spiky purple blob rolling across the land and being stopped at the fence and shooed away.

And after a while, the lockdown and fences and police hadn't been scary anymore. Just normal. Like the world had changed forever and no one really cared, because even still, the ones left living were all the same as always, with the same thoughts and stories that made them them. And the birds kept flying and the rivers kept running and the rain kept raining and the world kept going. Some said better than before even, because while everyone was locked down there weren't so many planes and cars and trucks and machines and factories polluting the air, and the earth started trying to heal itself, little by little.

And when it was over, all the governments had got together and pledged that from now on, no sickness would ever be allowed to cross borders again. Not country borders. Not state borders. Not city borders. Not town borders. Not even suburb borders. And the towns were all marked into zones, fences ready to go up, all over the world, and everyone had said it was good, that pledge. No one had talked about being the ones locked in with the sickness. *Sacrificed*, Phoenix thinks now. *This we choose to do …*

'We'll be okay, Phoenix. They are delivering food and supplies for everyone by drone and there are enough adults around to help if we need help. We'll be okay. We're good at looking after ourselves.'

'What about … Walter?' Phoenix can't look at Scarlett as he asks. Part of him doesn't want to know.

Scarlett takes a long time to answer. Too long.

'He's … sleeping.'

Phoenix looks at her, eyes sharp.

'The doctors have … what did they say? Put him into "enforced hibernation", they called it. It's like they've put his body on pause. For Walter, it's like no time is passing, his body and brain and everything have been … paused.'

Phoenix thinks of the toads that freeze themselves during hibernation. They stop their hearts beating and their blood flowing, and when the weather warms, it all starts up again. It's how they survive winter. He wonders if that is what they are doing to Walter. Freezing him somehow. Waiting for the warm.

'They said it was for the best. They said it will freeze the virus too and stop it getting worse, and there's a machine helping him breathe and his brain activity is all perfect and normal, and Gran and Josie are right there with him so he won't be scared when he wakes up. And it won't be for long. Just long enough for them to finish their tests and work out what's wrong and how to fix it. He's young and strong, our Walter. He'll be fine.'

Phoenix thinks that Janey was young and strong too. But maybe, maybe Janey didn't have time for enforced hibernation. He hopes she wasn't scared.

'And Gran wants us to put together a box for Waltie. Of all his favourite things, so they can talk to him and read to him, and so he can have them close by. She said to leave the box at the door in one of the yellow Iso bags in the cupboard, and to mark it *Outgoing* and one of the guards will come past to collect it. The doctors say it could help.'

Phoenix pulls Splinky out from under his shirt where he kept him safe from the rain, and all the girls cheer and clap, as though a small octopus made from socks will make everything alright.

An alert lights up Phoenix's phone and Horizon flashes blue and red and the Mickey Mouse voice calls loudly from the front window:

ADVICE FOR DISEASE OUTBREAK IN YOUR WATCH ZONE: HOME

YOU MUST ACT NOW TO REDUCE THE SPREAD OF DISEASE. FOLLOWING ADVICE WILL SAVE LIVES.

IF YOU ARE UNWELL, ALERT AUTHORITIES. ALL PEOPLE IN AFFECTED ZONES MUST STAY INSIDE UNTIL FURTHER NOTICE.

ALL ESSENTIAL ITEMS WILL BE PROVIDED FOR YOU.

POLICE WILL BE ENFORCING COMPLIANCE WITH THESE RESTRICTIONS.

PAY PARTICULAR ATTENTION TO SYMPTOMS IN CHILDREN. ADULTS WHO ARE ASYMPTOMATIC MAY STILL CARRY THE DISEASE.

Phoenix puts his phone facedown on the table and picks up the empty shoebox. Frankie has decorated it with pictures of bears and foxes and fairies flying on the backs of birds and written *WALTER!* in a rainbow of colours. All together, they head to Walter's room to find things to fill his box.

I heard bout this from history but I never seen it. Screens that show things like they's alive.

'Ohhh,' I say, and reach out to the screen showing Katie's face. It's perfect. My fingers hit the flat screen, but my eyes tell me she's here in front of me. I back away again, peek around the other side of the screen through the bubble where she still sleeps frozen in liquid, then back at screen-Katie.

She looks bout nine or ten and has smooth dark hair in two cute, blunt-ended pony tails. *'I'm Katie Su,'* she says in a small voice, and coughs. She holds the toy white kitten up. I turn around, coz my ears can't believe she's not here in the room with me. *'And this is Snooty Snowflake. He's got a turned-up nose like he's Snooty, and he's white like snow. I've never seen snow but Dad says he'll take me up the tallest mountain he can find when I wake up. I like art, and I like to dance, well, before I got sick I liked to dance,* and I like flowers. I don't want to go to sleep but it won't be long, just long enough for them to finish their tests and trials and then they'll know how to fix me. When I get home I want to learn to dance again and I want to learn how to make paper flowers, and do more collage art and go to the snow.' Katie smiles and I dunno her but she looks sad to me and her skin is blotchy. There's a bit of a red rash running down one side of her neck.

I should leave. My heart won't slow. Not with Katie sitting there staring out of that flat screen at me like she's alive and can see me. No one said screens was so real-looking. It's like there's a Katie right there!

The other bubble kids, they've all got names. The next one along is Jordan Maiava. My road is called Maiava Drive. All these kids is famous kids. Is that why they's here? Is this a weird graveyard for famous kids from olden times? Jordan looks so sad, lying there in the bubble. Not peaceful like Katie. His skin is a strange grey colour. I don't like it.

I move back to my friend Katie, with the good art and the fluffy cat, and hit the interactive button. Katie's head appears on screen, not attached to her neck, just her head on black and it's not quite as real as the first picture but it's even more terrifying, just a floating head.

Her skin is super smooth and her eyes all glassy. She is much brighter. *'Hi! I'm Katie, ask me anything,'* she says. Her voice is super fun, not sad and weak like before. How weird.

'Well?' she asks and her head tilts forwards. *'What do you want to know?'*

Can she see me? 'I wanna know everything,' I say.

'Try phrasing that as a question,' she says. She can hear me!

'Can a frozen girl answer questions?' I ask.

'I can!' she says and laughs. A strange fake laugh.

This is too weird. It's not a real Katie at all but a pretend Katie that talks.

'Why is you frozen?' I ask.

'I'm asleep for now, but I'll wake up soon.'

'What do you mean for now?'

'When the doctors find the cure they'll wake me and all my friends up.'

'But you was frozen more than a hundred years ago,' I say.

'Yes, that's right. In November 2029. They'll wake me up soon and I'll go home.'

'Where's home?'

'We have an apartment in the city,' she says.

'The city is dead.'

'Try phrasing that as a question.'

'Is the city dead?'

'We are not dead. We are asleep.'

'Is your parents frozen too?'

'No, the virus only affects children. Adults don't need to be hibernated.'

'Then maybe your parents died of old age?'

'I'm eleven years old.'

'The world is a whole lot different since you was eleven,' I say.

'Yes, there will be a cure and the world will be different but more normal. It won't take long for them to run tests and for science to discover a cure.'

I shake my head. 'Science makes new discoveries all the time, but important things. Environmental things. We live simple lives upon this honoured earth now. You see, we, I mean, you ... nearly destroyed it, and it nearly destroyed us. I think maybe that was just starting when you got frozen.'

'Try phrasing that as a question.'

'You're not really Katie, is you?' I ask.

'I'm a simulation using Katies's face and Katie's voice to answer basic questions. I can also have simple conversations.

I think it helps Katie's friends and family and other children curious about hibernation to be able to talk to me.'

'I'm sorry, Katie, they stopped coming to see you a long time ago.'

'Try phrasing that as a question.'

There's a whoosh, and the door slides open. 'What are you doing?' the old man asks.

He's back! His pale blue eyes is wide and his dark-tanned forehead is making a dirty-creased frown.

'I'm sleeping,' Katie answers.

'Nothing!' I say, and back away.

Phoenix wakes to a pained heat that stretches across his skin. It's the rash from his stomach, spread all up his neck and across his cheek. He watches the snow swirling madly in his snow dome of the North Pole that his mum gave him one Christmas. But why is the snow swirling when no one is there to have shaken it?

Wolfy stands by the window, his tail wagging and chin lifted as if in greeting the day. And when Phoenix tries to rise, tries to reach him, the world tips dangerously on its side and Phoenix suddenly realises that he is sick. Really, properly sick.

He looks across the room at Walter's empty bed and stumbles to the window, opens it wide, dragging cool air into his burning lungs, across his raw skin. 'I don't want,' he whispers to Wolfy, 'to leave.'

He doesn't want to go to the hospital. He doesn't want to be paused or frozen or forced to hibernate. He doesn't want to dream. Phoenix is more scared now than he has ever been.

An update lights up Phoenix's phone, and from downstairs Horizon announces to the empty kitchen:

ADVICE FOR DISEASE OUTBREAK IN YOUR WATCH ZONE: HOME

YOU MUST ACT NOW TO REDUCE THE SPREAD OF DISEASE. FOLLOWING ADVICE WILL SAVE LIVES.

IF YOU ARE UNWELL, ALERT AUTHORITIES AND STAY INSIDE. SYMPTOMS INCLUDE FEVER, HEADACHES, EXTREME TIREDNESS AND A RASH. IF YOU OR SOMEONE YOU KNOW ARE EXPERIENCING ANY OF THESE SYMPTOMS, OR IF A RASH APPEARS, STAY INSIDE AND CONTACT AUTHORITIES IMMEDIATELY.

It wasn't lice bites after all.

And all around him, the Ravened Girl of the bog whispers in winds that swirl the leaves from the trees and scatter them over Phoenix, as if he is in a snow dome of his very own. And he wishes then that he had stayed at the bog, with the quiet of it holding him still. He wishes he could run there now, wrap his arms around his mum's tree, sleep in the lap of her remembrering memory-orial seat and have her watch over him. He wishes he could feel again his skin become bog, wishes he could walk himself into its cool darkness.

He is so, so hot. He tries to call for Scarlett, but no sound comes out. He shivers and shakes and his body feels like it is splintering off into thousands of puzzle pieces, fallen to the floor.

The room spins faster and faster and everything turns to black.

'I din't touch nothing!' I say.

'You shouldn't be awake!' he says.

Awake? He thinks I'm a frozen kid?

'I'm just visiting Katie here,' I say, coz she said that was a thing that used to happen.

The old man though, he's looking around like the walls have ideas bout what to do with me. 'Where did you come from? This has never happened before.' He swipes up my *Security: Perez Stafford* card from Katie's bubble where I left it and turns and heads back out. 'Stay here!' he says, shuffling back out the sliding door.

I run for the door after him.

The floor is smooth, like my old work boots, and there's not much grip, but I run flat out and when it seems like I'll never make the gap in the sliding door that's getting thinner all the time, I just keep going and hit the edge of the door hard with my hands then my body. I shove my boot into the little gap and the door stops, hard up against my boot. Just room enough for me to get an arm through. No more.

'Wait!' I yell, but the air's already gushing, then the outer door slides open and shut.

The old guy drops the card on the table as he hurries off through another door. Is there someone else here? Has he gone to get them?

I pull my foot out of the boot and get a good grip on the door, try hauling it open. It won't budge. I'm trapped! What if he never lets me out? What if I never get home? No one will ever know what happened to me! And Da, he won't have anyone!

I've done it now! I shoulda told Davy. Left a note maybe. A letter to You!

The whole doorframe is blank cept for a beeper panel like the one that beeped to let me in here. There's nothing to let me open the door. Lights flash over the back of the room full of children in eggs. It's another door. I run over there. There's another glass room and another beeper panel. I need the card!

'Gah!' I'm burning-hot angry at myself, getting trapped. There's no way out. I run down the rows checking the ends of the eggs for tools. One of these kids is gonna have to be into woodwork or something and have a hammer in their case, then I can maybe bash my way out through the glass. That might be my only hope now.

'Shelby?'

What? I spin around. Clinging to the top of the stairs, his forehead shining with sweat, is my best friend. It's my Davy! I'm saved!

'Davy! Here!' I call and run to the front of the room. There he is, my best friend in all the world! He din't desert me! I've never been more glad to have a friend like Davy. I slap the glass and point at the table. 'Get the card. Bring the card to the door!'

Davy takes a few slow steps into the room. 'Why is you in there?' he asks. His beautiful dark eyebrows is peaks and his face is all worry for me.

'Bring me the card!' I jab my finger at the glass. 'On the table. The card opens the door!'

Davy grabs it by its cord and brings it to the door.

'Wave the card over the little panel thingy!' I say, and the door beeps and slides open. I wave Davy in, and he pushes the card into my hand through the crack in the door being held open by my boot.

'You're a dope, Shelby Jones, to lock yourself in here. What if I din't follow you?' Then the door behind him slides shut and there's that gush of wind that makes him squawk and jump.

'I din't lock me in. He did,' I say. The inner door slides open.

'The old guy?' Davy looks around.

'Yeah!' I turn away and run flat out for the new door I found at the back of the room.

'Shelby! Let's go!' Davy calls.

'I gotta see what's in here.' I beep the door panel and stumble in. There's screens everywhere. Screens and screens. A screen for each pod. Each child's name written over the screen: *Katherine Su, Jessica Tan, Jordan Maiava*. Names from our streets. Katie's screen is flashing red. *Hibernation fluid destabilised. Replace or start wake up procedure.* Jordan's screen says *Patient deceased.* Two other screens say *Patient deceased* too.

'They's dying?' I ask.

'What?' Davy is at the door. He's picked up my boot on the way. 'Let's go!' he says, looking over his shoulder.

'They's dying, Davy. I think they's dying,' I say.

'You think they's alive?' he asks. 'They can't be alive. They's frozen!'

'*They* think they're alive. Go push a button and ask one.'

'What?' Davy asks.

'Push the button at the end of the egg pod. Ask them if they's alive and wanna wake up.'

Davy frowns and throws my boot at my foot but he goes back out and kids' voices fill the room. Davy's pushed a lot of buttons at once and they's all talking.

'Shelby! They look alive!' he yells. His eyes is wide. He's looking from face to face on the square screens, standing against the wall like he's afraid they'll come out of the screens and grab him.

I slide the card into my pocket, pull on my boot and try to understand what all the screens in this new room mean. I can't. This is hopeless.

Davy's back at the door, eyes wild. 'These is all the children from our streets. These is all the children who died before the cities was abandoned. They can't still be alive!'

'They's not *all* alive.' I point to the message on Jordan Maiava's screen.

The old guy's back, standing in the doorway behind Davy. Blocking our exit. Davy scoots over behind me. We're trapped.

There's tears in the old guy's eyes. 'Mum said I had to look after them. Keep the power going, keep the machines working to keep them alive, but some of them have died. I don't have any more fluid. The batteries are old and dying. I don't know how to keep them alive. I need a doctor to help me wake them up.'

'We have a doctor,' I say. 'Back over the hill, where you got the chickens and the sheep at our township. Down there is a doctor. Dr Geraldine. You need to go get her,' I say, hoping he'll leave again. Stop blocking that door looking like he's gonna do something scary.

The old man blinks at me. 'I woke Jordan. The machine said to wake Jordan. But it was too late. The fluid went bad. Jordan couldn't breathe. Mum didn't say what to do if the machine couldn't clear the airways. The machine is meant to clear the airways, it's meant to happen automatically, Mum said.'

'I'm sure you did your best,' I say.

'But you're alive.' The old guy looks us up and down.

I nod. 'We're not city children, we're township children. We live near the doctor,' I say. 'Over the hill to where you got the sheep.'

But he walks on into the room with us. We back away. Try to figure out how to get past him.

The old guy turns and stares at Katie's flashing screen. Then he leans over. I scooch away from him, thinking he's gonna grab me, but he swipes at something on the screen, touches numbers. The screen goes green.

A woman speaks out of the ceiling. *'Wake up procedure initiated. Please have respiratory medical staff standing by.'*

'What?' I ask.

'You get that doctor,' the old guy says. 'I don't go near townships. Mum told me to stay away from them. This is a secret project. We have to get Katie out. We have to get them all out.' He hits more words on the screens and more screens flash green. The woman's voice echoes, stuttering now. *'Wake-up proced— wake-up procedure init— wake-up proce— wake-up procedure initiated.'*

Davy grabs me and pulls me to him. 'We gotta go get help!' he says, and sidles us past the old guy.

'Will they believe us?' I ask, stumbling after him, out the door, down the stairs. My head's spinning. The kids is being woken up. What's that gonna do? Did we cause this? I'm stumbling after Davy all the way to the bottom of the stairs.

'We'll get the doctor to call the government,' he says. 'They'll send drones and doctors. They'll know what to do.' Davy's already at the entrance, checking all around for the tiger.

The square is empty cept for the raven. She screams, launches and flaps right at us. We duck. Her wings slap my head and she glides up to perch on the stair rail and caws again.

I look back up the stairs. 'But they already left them here. The central government. Just left them here frozen and slowly dying, Davy. Why will they come to help them now?'

Phoenix waits, wrapped in Gran's crocheted blanket, the carved bird held tight in his hand and his own box of things on his lap. The girls have decorated it for him, just the way they decorated Walter's box, but they have drawn trees and plants and the bog and a giant raven in red sneakers on it for him instead. Phoenix smiles at that, then tries to catch the sob in his throat.

His whole life in a box, he thinks. There it is. His snowglobe. His favourite fairytale book from when he was little. Wolfy's puppy collar. His photo of his mum and the girls. Gran's old pocket watch. The little gnome figure Charlie gave him last Christmas. His collection of rocks. And Frankie found their seed journal, shoved under a bed and covered in dust, and she put that in there too, even though it belonged to all of them. *Ticerat Family Seed Journal*, written in old-fashioned spidery writing. Phoenix holds the box tight to his chest.

'And look! A postcard came for you from Charlie. It was in the letterbox. Must have been there for a couple of days. Do you want me to read it?' Scarlett shows him a card, addressed to *You*. That was his and Charlie's joke. They'd done that ever since they were tiny and had become best friends at kinder and Charlie couldn't say Phoenix, so just called him You.

Phoenix nods, and Scarlett reads it aloud to everyone, but Phoenix is too tired to really hear. He misses Charlie. Has anyone let Charlie know everything that's been happening? Phoenix is glad Charlie is away and safe. He wishes he had the energy to text. Scarlett puts the postcard into his box with the rest of his things.

Wolfy leans into Phoenix, nuzzling and burying his snout in his arm.

'You'll be okay, Phoenix. The doctors'll look after you,' Scarlett says but she won't stop crying and Ida is brushing the hair back from his head and Frankie's nails are digging so fierce into his arm that he can already see the marks. 'Gran says it won't be long now, before they find out what's causing it. They've already started trialling the medicines to fix it. And the minute they do, they'll wake your body back up again. They'll bring you both home and we'll party for a whole week!' Scarlett runs her finger slow and gentle along Phoenix's cheek, along the heat of the rash. 'And we'll all be here waiting for you. Okay? All of us.'

'Bring me home,' Phoenix whispers, and a shiver starts shaking at his bones. 'I'm scared. I'm ...' What if they pause him and then can't undo it? What if they unpause him too soon? What if the rest of them catch it? What if what if what if ...

Scarlett chokes back a sob. Then she reaches into her pocket and pulls out their mum's necklace with the bog oak ring. She hangs it around his neck. 'You'll be home before you know it. I promise.'

In the corner of the room, Phoenix sees the Ravened Girl of the bog in the thickening of the shadows under the window. He feels her flit around the room, sees just an echo of her shape catching in the dust lit up by the sunlight streaming into the room.

He squeezes the wooden bird in his hand. The girl rises behind Scarlett, her ravens perched on her shoulders and all along her stretched-wide arms and covering the furniture. She opens her mouth and speaks to them all in the thrumming of the rain and the bursting of clouds and the flapping of wings and the warm of the sun on their skin, and the girls cock their heads to the side, as though they too can hear.

'Listen,' Phoenix says, and they turn to him, leaning closer to his lips. 'Can you … can you hear her …' Phoenix stops, his tongue too thick to push the words free and the only sound then is the sobbing of his sisters and the soft tapping of their tears against his blanket.

There is a banging on the door. Loud and harsh. They are there. They are waiting to take him away. Two men in their beekeeper suits and masked faces. They are carrying torches to guide the way to the fences. To the edge of the town.

Phoenix wobbles to a stand. Frankie gets his shoes, but he shakes his head. He can't stand the thought of shoes on his hot itchy feet. The girls gather him in their arms and hold him tight and he doesn't complain at how their touch makes his skin crawl and burn. Outside, thunder rolls. The full moon shines bright between the trees. An owl calls.

The hooded, masked men take Phoenix's arms. They lead him away from the house. Away from his family. Eyes watch from house windows.

Scarlett sings then. Singing him down the road. An old song sung to them all by their mum, a lullaby to sing them sweetly into sleep. Curtains along the street open. Their neighbours watching him go, all of them listening to Scarlett's perfect lonely voice. Phoenix thinks he hears someone beating a drum.

She is singing him slowly down the hill now. Step by step now. Their torches licking the dark. Here he comes now. Barefooted, fumbling… And the Ravened Girl of the bog sings too, in tumbling echoes of everything that has ever been and everything that ever will be. 'Listen,' Phoenix says to the men. 'Listen. Listen. Listen …'

Davy slides along the wall carefully, coz a few steps through the square we spot the old tiger asleep in a patch of sun on the other side of the garden. It lifts its head and grumbles at us.

I grab Davy's arm, and whisper, 'That old guy, he's waking up all those children. What if the doctor won't come?'

'We just have to convince her,' Davy says, never taking his eyes off the tiger.

'If she thinks it's me, that I'm lying here hurt, she'll come. Don't tell her bout the frozen kids or the old man, tell her it's me. Tell her I've broken my leg. Bring her here,' I say.

'You want me to lie to the doctor?' Davy asks.

'You can blame me. You can say I went in and hurt myself and screamed for help. You only came in here to see if I was okay, and that's the truth. You never wanted no part of this, Davy, but what if they all die? What if by coming here, I've caused all those kids to die for real? One lie, Davy, for me. You don't even have to come back with them. Just tell them to follow the road to the square. Please?'

Davy don't look convinced.

I punch myself in the leg. 'Look! I'll bruise myself, say I fell and my leg went numb so I thought it was broke. I can make it look so you don't even know bout nothing else. I'll say I found the old guy after.'

Davy takes a deep breath like he's working up an argument, then lets it go, and says, 'Okay, Shelby Jones. One lie.' Then he grabs my hand. 'Go kindly upon this honoured earth,' he says all formal like he might never see me again. He takes off jogging, looking back over his shoulder at that tiger, but not looking back at me. Me who asked him to be untruthful.

Behind me that raven caws, '*Ca ca caaaaooooow!*' like she's bossing me back. I dunno if I wanna listen to her. Nothing but trouble, that raven.

181

An ambulance is waiting for Phoenix just outside the fence. They lead him silently inside. The gate on the fence clunks closed and rattling chains are locked behind him. He can't hear Scarlett singing anymore. Only the tyres crunching the gravel on the road. The motor spinning. The world turning slowly, just as it always does.

Empty, darkened streets roll out through the rear windows. They pass the grocery store, the pub and the toy shop, all closed up and barred. The giant teddy-bear out front now wearing a mask. The plastic smelting factory, lonely looking now with no smoke puffing from its top. Then buildings and shops with lights on he doesn't recognise.

They do not follow the roads that Phoenix knows lead to the hospital. He wants to ask them where they are going. He wants to know, is Gran waiting? He wants to tell them to lay him next to Walter, so they can be paused and waiting together ...

He looks at the man next to him and opens his mouth to ask, but the man turns away. Phoenix squeezes the bog bird tight in his hand and lets the wood bite sharp into his skin. He knows. He isn't going to the hospital.

I go back up the stairs, past the raven that twists her head to eyeball me like an old grouch, and let myself in. I slide past the strange old guy. Keep my distance. I dunno bout this man. I know everyone on my seven hundred. We're a community. We care for each other. This man, he's got no reason to care for me.

'Where's the doctor?' he asks like I should have her with me already, just pulled her out of my pocket or something.

'It'll take a couple of hours for her to get here,' I say.

The old guy nods, looks at the ceiling, squints like he's adding up in his head, then nods again. 'Good. Should be right on time. Katie is already warming up.'

'What's your name?' I ask.

'Alle,' he says. 'I run this now, like my mother and her father before. My mum was a doctor, and her father too. They've always worked here, waiting for the government to find the cure and for these children to wake up.' He hurries to the next pod, checks some numbers on the side.

I follow, keeping the pod between us. 'But why's you still here? The city's closed. Someone should've come and taken these kids a long time ago.'

'Today,' he says. 'Today, the doctor is coming. My charms are working. I can't leave until the kids are safe.'

I nod. 'I've seen your charms tied to things. That's why we came here. Why din't you just come to our township to ask for a doctor?'

Alle nods happily. 'My charms are working. I can't go into the townships. Mum said. *Never go into the townships*, she said. We're not meant to be continuing our work in the city. It's secret work. *Don't go out until there's nothing left for you to do here*, she said.' He hurries along to the next pod and I follow again.

I nod. Nothing left to do? Did she expect that one day all these hibernating children would be gone? So then, woken up gone? Or dead gone?

'I saw the sheep your tiger took,' I say.

'Poor old Jules.' Alle shakes his head. 'Both of us are getting too tired.' He looks at me and leans across the top of the pod. 'That's why we gotta wake the children and send them back out into the world. I can't take care of them.'

'I'm sure the doctor will know what to do,' I say. 'How did you get a tiger?'

Alle frowns like he dunno. 'There were always tigers in the city. Jules is the last of them. I think they were just left in the zoo. My grandfather said they were good at eating rats. Not enough tigers to breed healthily though. They were always going to die out. It's all coming to an end.'

I lean over the capsule Katie's in, the fluid's bubbling. The pipes going into her mouth is pulsing now, pushing fluids around the inside of her body as well as the outside. She seems less pale. A strange cap has fitted itself around her bald head.

'They named a street after Katie,' I say. 'But we never learned this is what happened to her. I thought she was an adult who helped out when diseases ravaged the cities, and died doing it.'

'She's not dead. Just sleeping,' Alle says, and he runs to the next egg. 'They were my friends my whole life. Back when there were no other kids, just me, and I only had my sleeping friends to talk to. I've been waiting my whole life for them to wake up. Trying my whole life to figure how to help them. I can't work on the frozen virus. But if I thaw them just a little, run the fluids, I think I can cure them. I just need to find *Fagus silvariacies*, somewhere. I've looked and looked. But still, I can't wake them without help.'

It's hard to imagine Alle small, but thinking bout any little kid only having screens to talk to and no actual real best friend like me and Davy, that's sad.

He's pushing buttons and talking. 'Not long now, Maggie.' He turns to the next pod. 'Not long now, Jessica,' he says, still trying to comfort the kids. 'It's the glyco-proteins, you see.' He makes his hands into a circle. 'The virus hides from the immune system in them. But if we help the immune system break them open with the special lectins from *Fagus silvariacies* seeds,' he opens his hands up, 'then their immune systems will find the virus and kill it.'

'I see,' I say, though I really don't. Miss Drinkwater don't teach us big words like he's using. All I'm hearing is that he needs some fagus whatsit thing, to get into a circle thing, maybe a cell – Miss Drinkwater says we're made of cells – to cure these kids.

There's two rows of eggs. Ten eggs altogether, four of them lighting up and pulsing now, swooshes and sloshes of fluid, but not Jordan Maiava's egg. His is dark. Just a red light sitting on top of his egg capsule in a line of flashing green lights. There's a couple of other dark capsules in the next row too.

The room fills with the rhythm of beating beeps. Eggs pumping fluid, trying to bring their children around. All the sets of beeps rolling on top of each other in a multi-beep wave. It makes my head throb and my skin crawl, all these machines, all this noise. I just need to go outside for a while. Sit in the warm sunlight like the tiger, maybe wait for Davy and Dr Geraldine, away from this man who scares me. Why din't I go back with Davy? In adventure stories someone always gets into trouble when the friends split up. This time, I think it's me.

'Sorry, Jordan,' Alle says, running his fingers over Jordan's dim egg. Alle stops and looks at me like he's seeing me for the first time. 'Where are you from?'

'I'm from the egg farm.' I put two pods between us and check the distance to the door and touch the hard edges of the card that opens it in my pocket.

'There's not enough,' he says.

'Not enough eggs?' I ask.

'Not enough fluid, not enough power, not enough time left in me, not enough brains to figure it out, not enough anything to let them go on sleeping, and no *Fagus silvariacies* to cure them.' Sweat runs down his forehead and he's waving his hands around.

I nod. What can I say to calm him down?

Alle jerks his head to one side. He lets out a little moan and runs down the row. I lunge away.

The beeps. There's a change in the beeps! There's a gap! But that means …

Alle makes a choking sound and throws himself over an egg capsule. Another light is red, another capsule has gone dark. Another of his childhood friends is gone.

The ambulance stops at a grey cement building, surrounded by more fences and guards with their guns and people in suits and masks. They are waiting to take Phoenix inside. The shadow of the Ravened Girl flits across the path.

'Don't you worry, now,' they tell him. 'Everything will be okay.' Phoenix doesn't believe them. Not for a second. There are nursery rhymes playing over a loudspeaker. They are there to make him feel better, but it just sounds spooky. Like he's stuck inside those horror films Frankie loves to watch. 'Just relax.' They pat his arm with their gloved hands. Their plastic-wrapped boots crunch across the gravel path.

He does not cry out with the bite of stones against his skin, or shiver at the iced chill of the wind through his blanket. He searches the huddled, hooded masses for eyes that loved and delighted. For ears that turned to his call …

'Gran?' he says. 'Where's Gran?' The Ravened Girl's hand wraps and squeezes his own trembling fingers.

They lead him past a gurgling fountain and a statue of a woman pointing. Phoenix follows her point but can see nothing except the blackness of the sky. Gloved hands nudge his back, hurry him through big glass doors and into the building.

Bright lights flood his eyes. Grey walls and white tiles. The floor is too smooth. Too clean. They lead him into a room, bright yellow and full of lights and screens like a movie set. A plastic couch is nestled in one corner and there are bright cartoony pictures lining the walls. Everything is covered in plastic sheets. The smell of disinfectant stings his nostrils and blurs his thinking.

They push him into a tent propped up inside the room and lay him carefully down onto a metal bench. It makes him think of the vet's office and how they lift Wolfy onto the metal bench for his vaccinations and wipe it clean afterwards. Phoenix imagines them wiping this bench clean after … after what? Where will they put him? Does he stay here? On the bench? The whole time?

Faceless adults, masks and face shields all head to toe in white suits, just eyes behind plastic, reach into drawers – 'Here, hold this and squeeze as tight as you can, love.'

A smiley-face stress ball is pushed into his hand, and they take the wooden bird from his fingers and lie it across the top of his box.

His phone vibrates in his pocket. It'll be Charlie. Telling him some facts about ravens or toads or asking if he got around to watching the latest Marvel movie yet. *Charlie.*

'Would you like some water? Some juice? What about a hot chocolate? We can do that. We need to get your fluids up as high as they can go.' They take his temperature and chart his measurements. 'Can you state your name please?'

'Phoenix Malachy Ticerat,' he says.

'And your date of birth?'

Phoenix struggles to spit the numbers from his tongue. He is so, so tired and the words are so, so heavy.

'How old are you, Phoenix? When were you born? Can you tell us how old you are?' they ask again, their voices pitched high as though he is a little one. As though he can't understand.

'Twelve,' he says. 'How long will I hibernate?' It takes him a few goes to get the words out loud enough for them to hear.

'Never mind that, now tell me about these things

you've brought in that box, Phoenix. That was good thinking,' a nurse says. She takes his phone from his pocket and puts it with his things. 'Is this your favourite book? Which story do you like best?'

Phoenix knows she's just trying to keep him calm. 'I want ... Where's Gran? Where's Walter? I need to be with Walter.' But the words aren't coming the way they are in his head, and they're tripping over each other in a meaningless babble, faster and furiouser, and the Ravened Girl flies faster and furiouser around the room, her shadow flipping and flashing across the grey walls, across the white tiled floor, and he tries to follow her, tries to see, to call out, until they push him down on the bed and tell him to hush.

'Shush now. There, there. Everything will be fine. I want you to focus on your breathing now. Can you do that for me? Like mindfulness at school. You do that at school, right? Four counts in ... hold ... and six counts out. Annnnd again. There now. You'll be fine. You won't even notice a thing. Like blinking. You'll blink, and everything will be better.'

And he knows they are lying.

They put music on. Bright loud music that is too bright and too loud and they bring out a razor, buzzing in their hands, and he knows what is coming. He does not struggle when rough hands hold the blade to his skin, and slice clean through his hair. He leans into those unknowing hands, yearning for one last touch of skin on skin ... 'Your hair will grow back, Phoenix. This is just to help the monitors ... just relax now ...' His hair falls like feathers to the ground.

They undress him then, painting his body with blue lines that hook up to a thrumming machine. *Drums beat faster now. Feet stomp. Stomp. Stomp. Stomp.* They strap monitors to his arms and the straps are cold on his skin *Ropes tighten.* His thighs and feet are gently bound with a seatbelt. 'Just so you don't fall off. Just relax now ... Here. Have some of this medicine, to help you relax ...'

He is hushed by the air thin in his lungs, by the drink, foul and bitter, poured on his tongue, in his mouth, down his throat. They bring out a helmet, skull-shaped and skeleton-bare, wires sticking from it like vines. 'We're going to put this helmet on you now, Phoenix. This will chart your brain waves. So we know you are okay.' They tighten the skull around his head, twist by slow twist ...

He tries not to panic. 'Mum,' he whispers, but the sound does not leave his lips.

Everything is turning fuzzy. The giant raven is

standing next to Phoenix's bed again, crying great big tears that rain down on the doctors and nurses and they wipe the wet from the foreheads and someone comes in with a mop to clean up the puddles forming on the floor. *'Krrrkrrrkrkkr,'* he whispers, and shakes his head and looks so very, very sad.

They place a needle gently in Phoenix's arm. 'I need you to take deep breaths now. As deep as you can, and you'll be back with us before you know it. Here, how about I read to you from one of your books? Let's see now, that's it, keep breathing, ah – here's a good one, *Once upon a time, there was a King and a Queen …'*

The room is filling now, with falling snow and floating feathers and flapping flying ravens, and the Ravened Girl flits in and out of the masked masses, wrapping him, holding him.

He is not alone. And he thinks how glad he is for his gift. He wishes he could tell Gran. Phoenix takes a deep breath. He blinks, long and slow.

'The King and the Queen were known far and wide for being the most gracious and kind rulers ever to rule the land. But the King and Queen carried a deep sadness inside of them …'

A clock is ticking on the wall. Phoenix imagines

himself deep inside the sound. Becoming the tick … tick … tick … of the clock. Entering time.

'For more than anything, the King and the Queen wanted a child of their very own …'

His eyes are rolling now. Voices whispering his ears now, on his tongue now. He is the messenger of the living and the speaker for the dead.

'Until one day, an old woman entered the kingdom,' Phoenix whispers.

'Hush now. Breathe nice and slow.'

His eyes close. The words on his tongue tremble and fade. The voices in his ears turn to nothing but the slow beatings of his heart. Everything feels so very, very heavy. And cold. Like Phoenix's blood has turned to mud and … He can't feel his body. Can't feel the air in his lungs, his throat. He can't hear the woman telling the story anymore, or the doctors talking or the clock ticking anymore, and he wonders if the clock has stopped. He wishes he could still hear it. It was nice to concentrate on the sound.

The Ravened Girl is close to him now. Even with his eyes closed and his mind slowing, Phoenix can feel her flitting, skitting, skirting, spinning closer and closer until she is surrounding him, embracing him. His skin tightens and her shadow presses closer, sinking, becoming. And she is there, inside of him. Inside his head, hearing with his ears, feeling the blood running through his veins, and he is inside her head now too. The warm touch of her mother's hand brushing her brow, the rumble of her father's voice. Stories told. Steps walked. Trails followed.

And now they are entangling further, dipping in and out of existences together. They are the breath of a babe, the gentle cough of an eldered man, they see through the eyes of children, and hear through the ears of the gods. They are paw prints and growing roots and hardening peat. They run with the wolves and soar high with the owls. They burrow deep, and sleep. And when Phoenix opens his mouth and whispers, all the flowers in the world blossom and bloom.

Here he will stay. No longer quite a child, and not yet quite an adult, in the place between this world and the next. Here he will stay. Not quite dead, they say, and never again quite living.

Can you hear him? Can you? Listen ...

Alle wails. He's mumbling at the kid in that capsule. A desperate, quiet chat through the lid glass as whatever's left of the child dies.

I don't wanna go over there. I don't even wanna be here. The soles of my feet burn, telling me to get out. My brain swirls. Confusing ideas. Stay, help, run, Davy will be back soon, you can help, you dunno how, get out, it's kindly to stay. So I'm just this mess of a person standing there, ready to bolt, ready to help but doing nothing kindly at all.

Alle stands and wipes his eyes on his sleeve, and once more goes around checking each of the flashing green-lit eggs. Fussing over pipe connections, the numbers on the side, then running to the back room. I dunno what happened when he tried to wake Jordan, or what went wrong with those other eggs, but he looks like he's thinking it's all gonna go bad again.

Maybe it will.

'When the doctor comes, we can take them from the capsules one at a time. She'll be able to clear their lungs,' Alle says to the screens or to himself. 'One at a time.'

I follow him to the room. 'Stay calm, Alle,' I say. 'Try to remember what your ma told you bout how the machines work,' I say.

'The equipment is old. The fluid is old, I can't get replacements.' Alle looks like he might cry.

'Can you call a drone to bring more supplies?' I ask, coz maybe he's got replacements before and the government does know he's here taking care of these kids after all.

Alle stops what he's doing and looks at me like I'm the one who dunno nothing. 'The drones stopped flying over last year. The central government shut down.'

I laugh. 'No,' I say. 'They's still there.'

'The pomegranates who come to look for bits and pieces, I see them on the edge of the city sometimes, they told me the government's finished.'

Now I know Alle is dreaming. Pomegranates is ancient fruits that nobody grows or even has seeds for anymore. I was worried for a second he was right, coz we've not seen any drones for ages, but I reckon he's been left too long on his own and his imaginings have all run wild.

'Pomegranates talk to you?' I ask.

Alle shrugs. 'They salvage stuff.'

'*Pomegranates?*'

'Townships are finished,' Alle says.

I shake my head. 'No, they's not. We is the generation that waits inside our townships for the earth to heal. We is the kindly folk.'

Alle nods. 'Kindly,' he says, and smiles. 'The earth is healing. It's time to be kind to it. What's your name?'

'Shelby Jones,' I say. 'I'm an egg farmer.'

'Today you're hatching kids not chickens, Shelby Jones. Go look at Jessica's lips,' he says like his head just cleared.

I nod, surprised that Alle is suddenly bossing me round like he's a proper adult, and hurry back along the rows. Reading the names, looking for Jessica. Bodhi Walker, Maggie Jensen, Jessica Tan. She looks the same age as me. What will I say to this girl if she wakes up and looks at me? I mean, Alle's not making sense with his talk of old fruits.

Her lips is pink. She's starting to look alive. 'She's good!' I yell.

'Now check Katie,' he calls.

We can get through this if Alle keeps knowing what to do like this. And Dr Geraldine will come and Alle will make sense and tell her how the machines work and these frozen kids won't die after all.

There's one more egg capsule in this row before Jordan Maiava and then little Katie. I don't wanna set my eyes on Jordan again now I know he's dead. Did I know deep in my gut he was dead when I turned away from him the first time?

I'm watching the ends of the egg capsules as I walk back up to Katie. The next one along, which has a green flashing light over it, has interesting things in the case. A black feather, a lumpy book lying open with a pictures of sprouts and leaves and fruits, each page with a lumpy envelope taped to it with a picture of a seed drawn on it, a photo of a large family with a lot of kids. Three girls, two boys. I check the egg. I think it's the bigger boy from the picture. He's older than in the picture. There's another picture of just him and a brown dog, a bit older. It's hard to tell with the strange cap now pushed down over his head in the egg.

His hands twitch like he might be dreaming of pulling it off or trying to pat his dog. I open the case at the end. 'It's no use. I've checked already,' Alle calls to me.

'Checked what?'

'The seed journal. It isn't there.' He's definitely confused, coz it's right here. What's he mean it isn't there?

There's a phone almost like the one the doctor used that time I was little and she had to phone bout my and Davy's coughs. I daren't touch it. 'Phones is delicate and they's the only way to contact the government to get the things we can't make, like medicines and lab testing for strange coughs,' she told me. And next to that is a carved wood raven, made to look as real as the one I fished out of the trough. What is it with ravens everywhere? There's also a card with a illustrated letter P on it, and inside the shape of the P is the outlines of lots of tiny animals and someone has coloured each little animal in with lots of pastel colours.

There's spaces for other bits and pieces and it makes me wonder about the posies tied to the rusty poles and bridges. Maybe Alle took stuff from this display. Maybe the snow globe or the rainbow disc belonged to this boy. Maybe all the things in the posies is things from these kids. I'd be mad if I woke up and all my special stuff was tied to poles and posies outside. If any of these kids do make it through this, Alle's gonna have to go out and bring it all in again!

In the egg, the boy screws up his eyes and his hands is still stretching open and relaxing, open, relax, like little shocks is making his fingers straighten. I call out to Alle, 'This boy's hands is twitching!'

'Which boy?' Alle asks.

I read his name. 'Phoenix!' I call. Then I say 'Huh?' Coz his last name is Ticerat, like our Walter Ticerat Community School. And P of the postcards? Is this why he has that wooden raven? Is this the You kid who the postcards were for that Alle's been leaving around? Letters bout a raven, and the end of the world and listening to a girl sunk in a bog?

'Can you hear her as she calls for you? Listen, listen, listen,' I whisper to Phoenix, just like the letter.

A blur of black movement catches my eye. Through the window, out on the white seats, two ravens settle down to wait. 'Oh …' I say as their pale eyes look back at me. 'Ohhh.'

A pain jolts through the stillness. Tugs at Phoenix's fingers. Pulls at his being. He tries to push it away, to focus on the eyes he is seeing through, the breath of air in another's lungs, in the cold of a faraway wind, but the pain gets louder, stronger, brighter until all the other existences are thrust from his thinking and he is pulsing, like a string knotted too tight, like a body too small to hold its own blood. He wants it to stop, to drift back into that sleep.

Breathe deep, they said. He forces the air into his lungs. Big deep breaths. And the sound of his breathing is drowning under the blare of an alarm. A beeping wail that won't stop.

He is crying now, yearning desperately for the Ravened Girl. He wants to wander again through her memories. To dance with her bare feet on fire-warmed mud. To feast on meat dripping with juice. The juice is tangy and warm on his tongue still. And now the pulsing is spreading, up his arm, his chest, his neck, his whole body convulsing and he is screaming in fogs of pain and darkness that blot out the sun and cover the world in fear – and the bog water is covering, drowning, darkening and his limbs are tearing and his head is slamming, cracking, and he doesn't know if he is her or if he is him or if they are both or neither – he gasps and his mind is ripping in half, in more than half, in pieces, in thousands of fragments that catch on the wind and drift up up up and …

'Alle!' I call. 'The Phoenix kid's really thrashing around!'

Alle shushes at me, flapping his hand. 'He's just waking,' he says. 'Or trying to.'

'Is there any more kids here called Ticerat, any called Walter?'

Alle shakes his head like there isn't but groans, 'Walter,' like there is and he don't even wanna think bout Walter.

I probbly don't wanna meet anyone they'd name a school after, anyway. I mean, I like school, coz I can hang out with Davy and eat what his mas pack us for snack time and play handball, but honestly, all that time Miss Drinkwater spends teaching us bout wars and famines, racial tension, diseases, global climate change and the fall of the cities, all that stuff is pretty sad. I mean, we beat it all. On our seven hundred we're safe from all that.

Unless it's true the central government's gone. Is people allowed to leave their seven hundreds now? Is the people from the other townships good kindly people like us?

'Where's the doctor?' Alle asks again.

'Where *is* the doctor?' I mutter. Davy could have reached Dr Geraldine by now. I hope he's okay. I bet he told her the truth. Davy'd always tell the truth. Maybe she won't come. But Davy, he'd get my da then. Da'd come back for me.

Phoenix's shoulders jump too. They shove up to his skull every time his hands fly open. His feet jerk and his eyelids is flicking.

'Where's the doctor! I can't do this alone!' Alle wails, rocking on the spot, his head jerking as he looks from egg to egg, his dark grimy face getting darker. 'They're all gonna die!'

Oh no! I'm just a kid who's hardly ever met a new person in her whole life, and now I have a man who looks like he's been left out in a desert for a year pitching a meltdown in front of me. His face is sweaty and red like he's bout to explode. I should be calm and comforting and kindly but I'm looking round for places to run to.

'It'll be okay,' I call out. I wanna ask why he started

up so many machines before the doctor arrived but I don't think blaming him will calm him down at all.

He strides straight at me. His eyes is wild and his fists is shaking.

'Alle!' I say. 'It'll be alright!'

I don't think it will be alright. I think we're in a mess. But he's still striding right at me like he wants to kill me! I'm gonna be strangled, left here, and Davy and Da will find me blue and dead on the floor.

'Alle!' I scream so hard my gut leaps up to my chest, but Alle doesn't even blink his wild pale eyes!

My ears set up buzzing like they do when panic takes hold. I dive out of his way, scoot around behind the egg capsules, run down the row and around another egg, then pop my head up to see if he's close. He's not.

There's a whoosh of air. He's not even in the room. He's left! He wasn't chasing me. He was leaving. He's panicked and run!

I run to the sliding door. 'Alle!' I yell at the sound of bare feet slapping down the stairs. 'Get back here! These kids need you!'

The footsteps fade.

I turn back to the room full of eggs. A room full of sloshing fluids and beeping machines. Four flashing green lights now. Four kids being woken up. And only me to help them!

I don't want Alle back being all jumpy and scream-ing but I don't want be alone here either. At least he knew how the machines work.

I run to the little control room. There must be a way to shut all this down. To turn off the kids who don't have that fluid alarm thingy that made Alle wake them up. He said he could thaw them a little to treat them. He's been putting them back to frozen before. I have to turn off the sloshing and beeping and make the skull hats go back into the egg wall.

Katie's screen is still flashing red. Her alert was the one that sent Alle into a panic. She probbly has to be woken up. Jessica is flashing green, *Entering Stage 2*. Phoenix's screen is flashing green, *Stage 2 Complete*. Maggie's has gone grey now like Jordan's. There's a screen for a kid called Romy, and there's a flashing note saying *Entering Stage 1, Abort Procedure*. I'm not sure what pushing that will do, but I'm hoping it means I'll be stopping the wake-up, so I touch the screen words like I saw Alle do before. *Returning to Stasis* appears on Romy's screen. His green flashing light returns to a quiet steady green. I think I stopped it!

There's two more screens that have the *Abort* panel showing. I touch those too. I think I've put three kids back into freeze. I can't see how to put Jessica and Phoenix back into freeze, though. The *Abort* word isn't there. Maybe it's too late?

Then Kate's screen goes grey. The light above her egg turns red. The pulsing fluids stop.

The lights in her egg go out. The beeping stops.

Patient Deceased.

Oh.

Katie.

I grab the doorframe. Hold myself up.

My face goes cold and my mouth turns dry.

I only just met Katie, a pretend Katie in the screen, but still, I knew her, knew what she liked. That kid is gone now. She won't ever get to hug her toy cat, or make more bright and beautiful flowery pictures. More than a hundred years she lay here, waiting to be alive again, and now, nothing. It's over. Oh, little Katie.

My gut sinks, so heavy. My throat stings. I blink through tears. I should cry. Maybe I should run away. But Jessica and Phoenix, they's still flashing green. They's bigger kids. Their screens never flashed red. They got no one else.

But how can anyone be frozen for so long and still be alive? It's impossible.

They's good as dead.

I don't wanna be here.

My forehead is tight and hot. My ears buzz. My tongue is fat and dry in my mouth. I can't think what is the right and kindly thing to do.

I know why Alle ran away.

The pain has stopped. Phoenix stills. His heart is slowing. Slower and slower. His thoughts are harder to grasp. He is fading. Further and further, and he wonders if he ever really existed at all. Phoenix feels the himness drifting. Getting less. Becoming smaller. Until he is no more Phoenix than he is anything else … and there is a knowing happiness in that release. A relief that he has become part of everything, just as everything has become a part of him.

There is a light, like a star. And the very small piece of Phoenix that still exists knows what he must do. Knows there is only one thing to do.

Around him, the ragged, soggy cardboard wings of the angels slap at his skin. Their nail-bitten fingers tug at his hair and pieces of rotting angel flesh flake from their heads and fall around him like the snow that swirls in his globe. Water presses cool against his skin, and he thinks he must be in his snow globe.

Phoenix gives in to the pull, to the struggle, and heads towards the light.

I pull up a stool to Phoenix Ticerat's egg. Watching from that little control room meant Katie died alone.

Phoenix's defrosting is further along than Jessica's. She is still chugging away. Fluids sloshing. Both of them further than Katie got, but I can't see how they'll get all the way.

I don't wanna look at their stuff no more. I don't wanna play their screens and see them talk. I don't wanna take on all that hope they had for better lives, and then see them die. That's not gonna make this easy. So I'm just sitting here to be close so they's not alone when it finally happens. That's the kindly thing to do.

I think of the letter bout a girl being put in a bog, and here he is lying underwater, full of fluid, just like the ravened bog girl the letter was talking bout.

I turn to the two ravens perched outside the window. 'You two got any ideas?' I ask them, and one of them bounces along the seat, launches and flies off down the stairs. 'You better be going for help!' I yell at her. 'I can't do this alone!' My voice cracks and I have to take a few deep breaths. I have to keep it together. Phoenix here is almost certain to die but his last moments shouldn't be hearing someone yelling at ravens.

Will the raven in shoes come for him? Is that one of those old gods people believed in? Will I see him like Phoenix did?

Phoenix's skin is so pale, like it's struggling to thaw, like the blood is struggling to find ways through the cold veins. He isn't even twitching anymore. He's gone so still. Dead still. Is this it? The end?

The back of my throat burns and I swallow hard. I'm not gonna be any good if I'm crying.

'Phoenix,' I say. 'Phoenix Ticerat?'

Maybe his brain can make his body work if he just remembers who he is?

Jessica is absolutely still too. Her lips and skin colour is good, though, a definite contrast from the pale blue singlet and pants they all wear, so I'm here with pale Phoenix watching the fluid drain from his egg, and get pumped out of his body, waiting for the end.

The cover pops off the egg and lifts up. The tube going

into his throat has stopped draining liquid and now sucks emptily. He's lying here in front of me, real as anyone, wet and slimy. There's a smell like wet mud, which is weird. The floor in here is old but clean. I lift my boots, but they's just dusty. Where's the mud smell coming from?

The raven screeches from outside and I just bout fall off my stool. Noisy old bird! I run to the window. 'Shut up, you!' I yell very unkindly.

I check the stairs.

Where's the doctor? Why hasn't she come? I'm guessing it's two full hours since Davy would've told her I'm lying here with a pretend broken leg, or more likely, the truth. Why's no one come? Oh no ... what if Davy twisted his ankle or got et by a tiger on the way? What if help's never coming?

Those stairs lead down to the patch of sunshine at the bottom. I could leave. I could go look for Davy. I could go home and sleep in my own bed, wake up and go on with my life like I never knew this place existed. A deep dark secret like a rock in my heart. Heavy and strange.

There's no sign of the doctor. No sign of Davy. Not even any sign of Alle.

I go back and sit beside Phoenix Ticerat. No one should die alone.

His skin is the colour of Jordan's now. Grey and milky, not even as healthy as the pale blue of his singlet and pants. And then his eyes scrunch.

Is he awake? Maybe he's not awake. Maybe his eyelids is just doing jerky things.

His hands give one little pulse, his feet give a twitch, but his chest is still. It's not rising and falling like a sleeping person's. I would put my ear on his chest to listen for his heart but it's wet and my ears is still buzzing. I undo an arm strap and turn his cold hand over, push my fingers into the soft side of the wrist. There's no beat there, so I push my fingers into the soft bit of his throat, beside the windpipe. And now my heart is racing so fast, I dunno if the weak tapping I feel is my heartbeat or his. He's barely here at all. I don't think he's got much time left.

'If you wake, I'll promise to help you, but I am just an egg farmer. I'm not a doctor. Don't expect too much!' I try a jokey laugh. It's a croak. I sigh. 'It's okay, Phoenix,' I say. Even though it's not. Even though this boy has been abandoned by everyone who ever loved him, including Alle, who made a whole life out of caring for all these frozen egg kids. This boy has been abandoned by time. 'Phoenix,' I say. 'I'm here. Phoenix?'

Phoenix's chest heaves. I reach out to touch him, but something zaps me. Some kind of invisible force that burns the end of my fingers. His chest heaves again. His arms and legs go straight out like something's hurting them.

Gurgles rumble up from deep within Phoenix Ticerat.

'Phoenix?' I yell.

Something is wrong with Phoenix. The machines is trying to make him right, but Kate died with only machines to help. Jordan and Maggie died with only machines to help.

The sloshing noise behind me stops. I turn, just as the beeping slows and stops. 'Jessica?' I ask, just as the lights in Jessica's egg go out.

'Oh, Jessica,' I whisper. I leap over and pull at the cover of the egg. But I can't get in there to do anything. She looks so good, lying just in a puddle of fluid now, looks alive. How can the machines have given up on her? I din't listen to her screen the way I listened to Katie's, but this is still awful, making my throat lump up and burning tears push at my eyes.

'Jessica,' I say and tap my hand on the cover like I'm trying to get her attention. 'You ain't alone at the end. You're not alone. None of you have ever been alone in all these years. Alle was a friend to you all and he never stopped looking for a cure.'

Phoenix groans, he's twisting. The cords of his muscles, still for so long, shudder then jolt and rise from his pale skin like strings pulled tight.

I have to do something. *'Phoenix!'*

'*Phoenix!*' It's the voice that brings him back. Calling. There is such a sadness to it.

'Scarlett?' he tries, but the word sticks thick and heavy in his throat. His lungs are burning. They must be on fire. Every part of his skin is screaming and itching as though his body is covered in insects, their claws scrabbling at his skin, pinpricks of pain lighting him up.

Phoenix forces his eyes open. His lids are heavy and dull. *Frankie*, he thinks. But it isn't Frankie. It isn't any of his sisters. There is someone, though. A girl. Leaning over him.

Why is there a girl leaning over him? Where are the nurses? Where are all the people? The doctors? Where is Gran and Josie and Walter and his sisters? Where is he? He isn't in the bright yellow room he went to sleep in. He's in a dirty, dingy room with cracks in the walls and a broken windowpane and mould growing in patterns along the roof. He tries not to gag on the tube in his throat.

The girl starts talking to him then, waving her arms about, words coming so thick and fast that he can't stand the wave of noise. He turns his head, forces his heavy, thickened arms to cover his ears, to shut her out. He clenches his eyes tight. And that's when he remembers. She isn't a stranger, this girl. He has seen her before.

Phoenix opens his eyes. He looks again at the girl. She isn't talking now, just looking back at him, as though she too knows him. It *is* her, Phoenix thinks. *Just like in my nightmare.* Hair cut short and scrappy, and fierce eyes staring back. Stuck in a world that's strange and wrong but somehow familiar. Here she is. Waking him up. Holding out her hands to him. Did she dream him too? Did they dream each other?

Phoenix knows how this dream ends. With the world crumbling around them. With the end of everything.

My hand buzzes when I reach for Phoenix again. A weird tingle, a tingle so bad it hurts. Nobody ever survived in the egg. 'I'm not leaving you in there, Phoenix. I'm not leaving you in the egg to die!' I push my hands through the burn, grab his arm and yank him from the egg.

My arms zap straight and useless and Phoenix slides from the egg like *he's* made of egg. Slimy white and lumpy yolk, sliding over the edge and me thinking, *Don't let the yolk break!* coz I'm an egg farmer above all.

But if Phoenix's head is the yolk, it tears free from that skull hat. The tubes down his throat unravel out of him, he bounces off the stool and flops at my feet, mostly gooey white and not much yolk, but intact.

I stand over him. I don't wanna touch him, my hands still shaking from the last time I touched him.

'You okay?' I ask. 'You alive?' I ask. 'Phoenix?!'

He gags, he gasps.

'You's alive!' I say. 'Come on. Tell me it's true!'

Phoenix Ticerat rolls on his back. He opens his eyes and stares. He's staring at me like *I'm* the thing that's strange. Like *I'm* the one that don't belong here.

I wanna say both of us don't belong here, him more than me, but I don't coz he's holding me in his stare, and all I wanna do is make sure he's okay, so I kneel down beside him.

'The … end,' he croaks. At least that's what it sounds like he's saying. His voice is dry as sandpaper. He takes ragged gasps between each word. 'The. End. Everything.'

'But this isn't the end. You're alive. See? Alive.'

He turns his head and I lean to block out Jessica's dark egg. I hope he can't see that there's hardly any alive eggs left. I put my hand out to him, like we were shown in history, how people used to say hello with a handshake.

He lifts his hand and slides it into mine. It's wet, floppy and cold, but soft and so alive! I smile.

'Welcome back to the world, Phoenix Ticerat.'

The girl from his dream is babbling. He wishes she would slow. Wishes she would stop. But instead she keeps talking about eggs and yolks and whites and chickens and there are giant eggs everywhere, like the giant raven came and laid them all out in a line, and – that's it. He must be dreaming. No one real could talk this much and this fast about eggs. This must be the medicine, pausing his body and him just dreaming. He wishes the dream would stop. And why does the dream hurt so much? Dreams aren't supposed to hurt.

The dream girl keeps chattering about eggs, and slowly, slowly, his dream body is beginning to hurt less. Slowly, the blood warms the tips of his fingers, his toes start tingling and flexing on their own. Slowly his arms and legs aren't feeling so very, very heavy. He tries to wriggle his fingers, but nothing happens except a tiny twitch.

'You're not real, you're not real, you're not real,' he croaks, his throat burning. The dream girl stops mid-word. 'Probably?' he whispers.

She bends down and looks at him, so close that he wants to push her away. Like she's checking to make sure he is really in there. She pinches his cheek and it hurts. Real hurt. And maybe this isn't a dream. Is it? But if it isn't a dream, then doesn't she know he is sick? Doesn't she know to keep at least two arm-spans distance? And where is her mask? Unless, unless they have found a cure!

Is he awake? Really awake? Is that why they woke him up? He's cured? They're all cured? It's all over already? Just a blink of time, they said, and they were right! Cured! He's going home!

He closes his eyes, and feels the girl's fingers on his own, rubbing, gentle soft circles that make him think of his mum and the way she would rub his hands when they got cold.

'Hey, wake up! Up with the sun, there's work to be done!' the girl says then, and it sounds so much like something Frankie would say that Phoenix opens his eyes and smiles at this girl who maybe just really, *really* likes eggs. He laughs then, and the air is pouring from his lungs, filling the room, the laughing bouncing off the walls and raining down on them from every side. The laughing shakes his body, wracking it and tugging at his ribs. But when he stops, he feels fresh again. Whole. He wriggles his fingers, and this time they move. He's awake. Really awake. And he's cured!

'There you go! I thought you were trying to leave me again.'

Phoenix tries to answer, but the words stick and he coughs and gags instead. He looks again at the giant dark eggs, and the dingy room. 'Where?' he whispers, his throat scratchy and sore and his brain fugged. 'Where's Walter? Gran? Is Charlie back yet? Are they okay? Where ... am I?'

The girl turns white. She doesn't look at Phoenix.

I take a deep breath and nod slowly. 'You're Phoenix Ticerat, and your family member Walter was probbly really good at school since there's one named after him. Me, not so much. I mean, I'm pretty good at maths and lit, but apparently I ask too many questions in history, coz you know what? Miss Drinkwater just tells history that's not important, like wars and famines, and not important stuff like, oh, there's a derelict city real close. And that our streets is named after kids your age from the last great pandemic.' I'm talking too much, which is weird when there's so much I don't wanna tell him.

Phoenix scrunches up his face. 'School?' he asks, and frowns. 'My Walter?'

'Maybe your Walter. Who is he? Is he your dad? Did he discover the disease?'

'He's here?' Phoenix tries to look at the egg behind me.

I shake my head and look away. 'I don't think so. I asked Alle, the man who runs this place and ... I don't think so.'

'He's ... awake?' Phoenix rubs his head like all this talking is hurting him.

I shrug. 'Got better or still asleep, it makes no difference now. Is you hungry? Do you need some food or drink?' I look around. Alle must have something nearby.

Phoenix shakes his head.

'Can you sit up?' I hold out my hand to help him up. He lets me pull him up a little but lurches sideways and groans. I put him back flat. 'Probbly need a bit more time.' I pat his chest.

'No difference now?' He keeps repeating bits of what I'm saying. Little chicks hatch out of eggs and seem to know more bout the world than this guy right now. He must be so confused, but I don't think trying to tell him everything is gonna make him less confused. I need to start slowly.

'Well, you see, it's the *now* in that sentence that's the problem. You see, *now* the city has been abandoned and *now* we all live in groups of three hundred and fifty people on seven hundred hectares each. It's been that way for ages. No one lives in the cities anymore. *Now* we all live kindly zero-pollution lives. We look after the earth and the earth looks after us.'

'What?' It looks like he's gonna panic. His lips keep on moving, but it's as if he dunno what words to use.

I shake my head. 'You see, it happened before I was born. Stay here, I'll go see if Alle has a towel or something. You're wet and still so cold.'

I stand up, pull the swipe card from my pocket and run to the door. Alle must have a room close by. He wouldn't leave the kids alone at night.

'Girl!' Phoenix yells like he never learned my name. Oh, maybe he din't.

Another door lock panel opens sliding doors to a corridor, and the first door leads into a room with the sliding window long gone and a pipe coming down into a giant blue tub of water. There's cups and pots, and strange round red fruit with little knobs on the end. Pomegranates? Is this what they look like?

I get my face real close. 'Hello?' I ask them. But whatever they is, they's just fruit, and fruit don't talk no matter what Alle thinks.

There's a little stovetop in here, and faded towels and a mattress with a blanket. They'll do. I grab towels and a blanket and a cup of water, and go back to Phoenix.

When I get back, he's staring at Jessica's egg, mostly drained of fluid and dark with a red light sitting on top. Her little grey hand lies limp and near the edge he can see. He looks at me, his eyes full of asking.

I wrap one of the towels around his shoulders and set the cup of water beside him. 'Phoenix,' I say. 'I don't think you'll wanna hear bout any of this.'

But he just nods like he really does.

'Well.' I scrunch my eyes real tight for a moment so the sneaking tears squeeze out the sides to the outside of my cheeks. I wipe them away and take a deep breath. 'Well, you're the only kid in this room who's woken up so far. There's some other kids still frozen, but most of them died in their eggs.'

Phoenix pushes away from me like my words is burning him. Pushes across the floor and lies there blinking.

I sit down and wait.

He groans and it sounds like, 'What? What? Why?'

I shake my head. 'Listen, Katie, she was flashing red and she was gonna die, so Alle started her off, but then when he heard that we could fetch a doctor he started a whole pile more. He said you was all out of time, the fluid was going bad, but I turned three back off. Davy went for the doctor, but he's not come back in time and who knows

230

when Alle will be back. I was the only one who stuck around to make sure you ...' I stop talking coz Phoenix has his hands over his ears.

His body is kind of jerky sobbing like he knows something's gone horribly wrong. I put the other towel and the blanket around his body in case he's cold.

Finally he takes some deep breaths and looks at me again.

'Hi, I'm Shelby Jones,' I say, and smile, and he's just looking at the wet tears on my cheeks and in my eyes and not at my fake smile at all, so I keep going. 'Shelby was my grandmother's name. All my names come from women in our family going way back. I'm Shelby F—'

'Where's my family?' he whispers, interrupting my personal history lesson.

I run and get all his stuff. His photos and his books and the wooden bird. Now he's got everything familiar around him. Everything that's his. I've done my best to be kindly.

I push the photo of his family into his hands. 'This photo, Phoenix. This isn't how it is *now*. This photo was taken more than a hundred years ago.'

She's saying words, this Shelby, but they aren't making sense. Phoenix tries to slow the words down in his head. Concentrates on each one to try to understand it.

A hundred years. Isn't *now*. Isn't ... isn't ...

But the girl just tells him again about walking kindly on the earth and being the ones to take care of the planet and '... so that it can heal from pollution. So that we could heal from strange new diseases. Don't you get it? That sickness you all had. There never was no cure. We couldn't live in cities anymore. We had to live in isolated groups. It changed everything. It killed the children first. Suddenly there was a world with just about no one under thirteen. People panicked then. I never even heard bout freezing kids like this until I found this place. I don't think it worked out. No one else was woken up. Just you.'

That's when Phoenix understands. The rash. The fever. The lockdown. The virus. The dark egg coffins.

The school named after Waltie. Waltie who was too little to even make it to school himself. They said he was going to be paused. Just put on hold until they could work out how to fix him. But they never did. They never worked anything out at all.

And even though Phoenix understands what this means, that a hundred years have passed, that even if they didn't get sick, Gran, Auntie Josie, his sisters – none of them could still be alive, no matter what. His body turns numb. His brain can't think of him being himself, no older, and them being – dead. All of them. Gone.

He pulls himself up on an egg, and stumbles from one to the other, his hand resting on the black glass. Eggs, Shelby calls them, but he knows they aren't eggs. Eggs are for birthing. These are for dying. Even as he thinks it, he sees one of the last green lights turn from green to red. *Patient Deceased.*

There is a noise from the window, a flapping on the glass, and there is a raven, watching. He hears Gran's voice in his ears. *Eyes wide, Phoenix, eyes wide.*

Phoenix stumbles to the window, and his hand knocks a thick file from the sill. The papers flutter to the ground like feathers. And hanging from the window hook is his mum's necklace, the bogwood ring tied to the leather, like

233

it's been waiting for him this whole time. Phoenix hangs it around his neck. *Mum*.

Shelby gathers the papers all up on her hands and knees, reading bits of them as she goes. She talks more than Frankie, this girl, and a lump chokes Phoenix. *Frankie. Scarlett. Ida. Walter.*

'Must be Alle's notes and stuff,' Shelby says. 'His mother and him was working on a cure. He said something bout not having enough brains, but he's worked real hard on it. I mean, look at this! Museum notes bout people they found when the permafrost melted. Oooh, was there a museum here in this city? Will we be able to see it some day, do you think?' She flaps a paper before Phoenix can answer. 'It says here ancient people from thousands of years back had the same disease as you but somehow recovered. And … I dunno what this is, but Alle could really draw! They found a whole lot out bout it. Look, says here the virus was different for people with rare blood types. Like me! I've got the rarest blood type. AB. Says here that AB blood type can carry the virus but with no symptoms.'

Shelby starts laying the paper out like a rug and Phoenix wants to tell her that he doesn't care about any of it, because doesn't she get it? If they haven't got a cure, doesn't she know what this means? What if she gets the sickness now too? And even if her blood is rare, what about everyone else? It doesn't matter that they've been living in their three hundred or whatever, they'll all be dead without a cure, just like before. When they paused him, they paused the virus. When she woke him up, she woke up the virus too. But she doesn't seem to realise.

Phoenix slumps to the floor – and that's when he sees the drawing. Red and yellow exclamation marks are scattered around the page, and pinned to the corner is a letter from a *Farmerceuticals BioLab*. Phoenix picks it up, but Shelby grabs the drawing from his hand and starts reading the letter.

'That's how the ancient people recovered! Alle told me there's some kind of cell the virus hides in and sneaks around the bodies of children.' She makes her hands into a circle. 'But something in this seed makes the cell open.' She spreads her hands apart and makes her eyes wide. 'Then the kids' bodies can see the virus and kill it!' She smiles at me like I'm supposed to be impressed. 'Looks like the ancient ancient people from way, way back knew how to cure your virus! The only problem is, the cure is in this thing from a nearly extinct tree.' She points to a bit of text. 'A silver-edged beech tree nut. But it says the tree became extinct thousands of years ago, probbly. The planet is a few degrees warmer than your time, Phoenix. It would have been lost before you even.' She hands the page back to Phoenix and shrugs, going on about how cool-weather plants don't grow anymore, and is it true that there used to be more than three types of apples?

But Phoenix isn't listening. He's looking at the drawing of the seed. He knows that seed. It is big and black with a whorl in the middle like a fingerprint, and it is speckled with the most magnificent red he has ever seen. More like a jewel than a seed.

It feels to Phoenix like he buried that seed only yesterday, digging at the dirt with Wolfy, telling his mum to look over it. *A hundred years*, he thinks. A hundred years, and will it have grown? So much could have stopped it from growing. He doesn't even know if a seed kept in a bog *can* grow. But maybe … just maybe … He gives his mum's necklace a squeeze.

'The bog.'

'What bog? You mean the bog from your postcards? Oh. I dunno if you ever saw them. Probbly not. The ones that said they was to *You*? I found some and, I mean, I figured if they was to *You*, and I'm a *You* too even if I'm not the you meant—'

'We have to ... go to the bog.' Phoenix manages to spit the words from his aching throat, from his too-heavy, too-thick tongue.

'To your bog? But there's no bog on our seven hundred. Maybe there is a bog out here on the edge of the city down the river a bit. Miss Drinkwater says there was, but we was told swamps is where the worst pollution settled, the run-off from all around. It could be toxic still, and giving off gases that make people and animals pass out and get sucked under. This swamp's probbly full of the bones of dead people and their ghosts! And we need to wait for Davy and the doctor. They can help you. We can't just go without telling someone. It could be dangerous. Strange zoo animals and poisonous wreckage and wandering people. We're not allowed. I'm not allowed here even!'

Phoenix shakes his head and grabs at the blanket that's fallen to the floor and hoists it back around his shoulders, wrapping it tight around himself. 'No more people.' If the virus is still in him, they are all in danger. Doesn't she get that? Just like the reindeer thawing out from the ice and releasing anthrax back into the world. Here he is, thawed out and releasing the virus back into the world. He thinks of the sinkhole opening up and devouring the city whole.

Except now *he* is the sinkhole. That is a lot to be held responsible for.

And he knows very well what will happen if he waits. He has read too many books, seen too many movies to know what happens when someone comes back from the dead, or from outer space or from another time. He won't ever be listened to. They'll just want answers. All of them, asking him questions, poking and prodding and questioning the boy from the egg. Working out why he didn't die, when everyone else did. They'll stick him in some secret hospital and experiment on him … and they won't believe him about a seed planted a hundred years ago gifted to him by some ancient bog girl that a giant raven in red sneakers led him to.

But maybe Shelby will. If he can just show her.

He picks up the drawing and taps the seed. 'The bog,' he croaks, and her mouth drops open.

'This seed? Is at the bog?'

Phoenix nods.

'Is you sure?' she asks. 'The seed for Alle's cure?'

Phoenix nods again and tries to stop the shivering, shaking cold that is eating at his skin. He gives himself a moment, breathes deep and feels the energy coming slowly back into his body. He can do this. He has to do this.

Now, quickly, before this Davy and whoever else comes and takes him away to experiment on. Phoenix pulls himself up and staggers between the darkened eggs. He doesn't want to see their names. He doesn't want to recognise anyone. He walks like he's in a dream, his legs numb, crashing from one surface to the next. He fumbles and stops at the pile of his things, taking the seed journal and the carved raven, and then he pushes himself on again, not thinking, just putting one foot in front of the other.

He stumbles through one door and then the next and the seal whooshes to let him pass, and Shelby is yelling after him and calling him, but he keeps going. One more door, down a hallway—

'You's going the wrong way!' she says.

Phoenix stops. There is a display. Like the displays at the museum exhibit. *A Brief History of the Corvic26 Pandemic.* It's a timeline. He's walking backwards down the timeline, reading all about the *Introduction of the Townships* and government drones and kind folk and how they worked out that three hundred and fifty people living on seven hundred hectares was the perfect number for survival. And then he reaches his time.

Introduction of Suspended Animation.

Phoenix reads how they had been ready with the

technology, devised after the last pandemic, but no one was sure that it would work. He reads how clever they were, to be able to pause the virus, to suspend the children in enforced hibernation, to hang them between life and death, while they waited for a cure to be discovered.

He reads how the virus was transferred from the corpses of animals dead and buried for hundreds of years in bogs and ice, but exposed due to climate change. He reads how they think the virus came from a particular species of ancient corvids, similar to ravens. *Little Moon Eyes. Little Larry.* Didn't they think it strange how the virus had been in suspended animation, paused in the bog, for all that time before them too? Didn't they think about what could happen? *Is* happening? What is wrong with adults? Why don't they ever think things through?

He reads the names of all those infected with the virus. He reads his name. Walter's name. Scarlett's name. A list that goes on and on and on, covering the entire wall. Ida's name. The names of all the kids from his street, from his class. Of their brothers and sisters. A wall of the dead. Most of the names have a line going through them, as though someone has scratched them from the list.

Phoenix runs his finger along his family's names. He doesn't try to stop the tears falling. Scarlett. Walter. Ida.

Charlie is probably on another list somewhere else. In some other place. Some other zone. Poor Charlie, sick so far from home.

He searches for Frankie, his finger running up and down the lists. Frankie's name isn't there, isn't listed with all the other Corvic26 victims, and in one wonderful, brilliant moment, Phoenix realises that she survived. Somehow she didn't catch the virus. And he remembers that her blood type was AB too – like Gran's. Frankie wasn't put into an egg or enforced hibernation or anything. She didn't catch it! She wasn't sick!

'She's alive!' Phoenix starts, and then remembers. A hundred years have passed. Frankie might not have died from the virus, but she's not alive. Not anymore. And more tears fall, knowing how alone Frankie would have been. The only one left.

Shelby's shaking her head. 'They's all gone.'

Phoenix heaves one breath, and then another. He keeps walking, down to the very beginning of the exhibit. Sealed in a glass case is some black feathers and a little plaque that reads *Mummified feathers from a now-extinct rook carrying Corvic26*. 'Thirteen feathers,' he whispers and takes another step. *The First Known Case*, the sign reads, and Phoenix turns to look at the small person lying inside, their body laid out like an Egyptian mummy, their hand resting on an old octopus made from socks.

'Walter,' Phoenix gasps, and finally his legs give way.

Shelby is there then, rubbing his arms, holding him tight, shushing him, rocking him just like Gran would, and for a moment, Phoenix can pretend that none of this is true. He can close his eyes and pretend.

'I din't know,' she is saying, over and over. 'I din't know.'

Phoenix waits until the sobs stop shuddering in his lungs. Waits until he can gather the words properly on his tongue.

Phoenix pushes Shelby away then and looks down at his body. At the blue tinge that has tattooed across his skin. There is no rash anymore. He has no fever. But ... he looks at Shelby. He has to get her to understand. 'I'm alive.'

'Yes, you're alive,' she says. 'I'm sorry none of your family made it through with you. It's horrible to be alone, but everyone is real nice on our seven hundred.'

'The virus. It's in the bog like me in the egg like the raven like ...' Phoenix stops talking and tries to slow his words. To gather his thoughts. His head is so woozy.

He taps his chest. 'Is the virus still alive? In me? Is it alive now, in you too?'

Virus? Phoenix is staring at me so hard with his dark eyes all wet and red from crying.

I woke Phoenix up. Did I wake the virus up too? Did I release the virus back into the world?

I dunno what it is for sure. We don't get viruses on our seven hundred. We keep our hair short and wash our hands before we enter buildings and take off our shoes and we all had vaccines as babies and I never ever before met a new person, cept the baker's husband when I was six and he was healthy and delivered by the government drone to put our numbers back up to three hundred and fifty. Alle was my second new person ever and Phoenix is my third.

I look down at my hand that I touched Phoenix with and then I hugged him coz he just saw his little brother dead and exhibited like he was a thing and not a little kid whose family loved him. My heart almost stopped when I saw that kid in there, and then figured out he was the kid from Phoenix's photo! All this time I thought our school was named after a scientist who discovered the last pandemic. Not a tiny boy who was the first one infected!

We don't celebrate individual people, we celebrate what we do as a community. But the people who put the first streets into our township, they were from the olden times. And I don't like that they named them after sick kids, no matter how much they wanted to remember them.

'I dunno,' I say carefully. 'Do you have the sickness in you?'

Phoenix shrugs and he's looking around like someone will come and tell him. Someone who knows more than me. We both want that. I'm hoping for the doctor or even Alle right now.

Phoenix hauls himself up, wraps the blanket around his shoulders and takes a few deep breaths.

Maybe we did bring back the virus. But maybe we can stop it too. I dunno. Phoenix thinks he knows where to find the seed. How do we use it? I bet Alle will know and then the virus will be gone forever.

I stand up too. 'I can take you to the river. I'm guessing that could run down to a bog.' If we head back towards the river we're also heading back towards our seven hundred for the first bit, and maybe Davy and the doctor will be coming up the road and then they can take over. But I'm not gonna argue with Phoenix. He's having a real bad day. The worst day of anyone I ever met, and maybe it is really important to find this seed.

'Not too close. To anyone.' Phoenix points at one of the old signs on the wall. *HANDS! FACE! SPACE! Wash your hands, wear a mask and keep your distance! Help stop the spread. Stay apart, to stay together.* 'Hands, Face, Space,' Phoenix says. And then I get it.

If I've got the virus, I need to do all this stuff the sign says too. Stay away from Davy and Da and … I need to get me a mask.

'Walter.' And just like that, Phoenix takes a big deep breath like he's pulling up all his strength, then grabs an old chair and smashes it right through the glass. It clouds and explodes with a bang, pelting stinging chunks at us so it's like we're caught in an avalanche of glass rocks. I scurry backwards.

'That was not kindly!' I say.

Phoenix just rests with his hands on his knees like that heave took all he had, then he straightens up and stares at his little brother laid out like that, and he says, 'No museums. Pinky promise. Walter hated museums.' And he picks his way over all the broken glass chunks not even noticing the blood that's dripping from his foot. I stand there watching but there's no way I'm touching a hundred-year-old dead kid.

Phoenix picks Walter up and walks back to me. He looks at me, and he looks at Walter, and then, just like that, Walter breaks up in his arms. Turns to ash and dust right in front of our eyes!

I guess it's something to do with being out in the air, but I don't care why, now I'm all covered in a cloud puff of dead kid. I wait, staring at Phoenix, waiting for him to lose it. I would if that was Davy. But Phoenix looks at his arms. For ages. Like he's turned to stone.

Then he gathers up as much of that dust as he can, scraping at the floor with the sides of his hands, grasping at little mounds, and without asking or nothing starts filling up my pockets with his dead brother and it takes everything I got to stand there and let him do it.

There's a little thing made of socks, with eyes sewn on and stuffing poking out of some stitching. I bend down and pick it up out of the dead-boy dust.

'Splinky,' Phoenix says. He takes the dusty toy from me and hugs it hard.

I lead Phoenix back up the hallway and to the top of the stairs. He's a bit wobbly on his legs still. 'Do you need some help?' I ask. I wanna grab his arm and help him, but if he does have a disease and I already touched him three times and din't catch it, maybe I shouldn't touch him again and test my luck?

I grab my bag and hoist it over my shoulder and run back to Alle's kitchen room and grab a pair of slippers I saw there before. Poor Phoenix's feet is leaving bloody spots on the floor. Probbly soft from years of soaking then walking on glass chunks. He's not gonna be able to walk far, even if the soles of his feet is numb.

He slides his feet into the slippers, nods and grabs the handrail with one hand and jerky-walks on down the stairs, with me just ahead of him, my arms ready to grab him if he falls.

At the entrance to the building he sees the tiger and gasps.

But the old tiger is just stretched out sleeping in a patch of sun, his dull fur draped over his bones.

'I thought you saw tigers all the time in the olden days?' I say.

'Only in zoos!' Phoenix says.

'Probbly where his great-great-great grandparents came from,' I say. 'Not much tiger left in that one.'

Then Phoenix looks up at the sky. 'It's so blue.

So … big. The sky is so big and blue,' and I dunno what he's on bout coz it ain't that blue today anyway you look at it. But then he turns and looks at the city, and I can tell that what looked like an amazing spectacle of tall buildings and piles of interesting rubble and fascinating discarded bits and pieces of treasure to me and Davy looks like a nightmare to him. Phoenix's face gets even paler and his eyes go squinty like it hurts to look.

'What happened?' he asks, and waves a hand all around.

I shrug. 'I don't think nothing big happened. Was just abandoned. Nobody can live in cities now. No one could travel coz of spreading viruses and causing pollution. So it was all just left to ruin. Come on,' I say. 'The road to the river is this way, don't mind the old tiger.'

Phoenix walks real slow, too-big slippers scuffing, that Splinky thing dangling from one hand and his seed book and wooden raven in the other. Like they's all he's got left in the world. I guess they is. I don't think he should be walking at all after years of his muscles being frozen. But he's looking around at the old city like it just fell down yesterday and it's all a surprise. Maybe it is to him. His colour comes back the further he walks, though.

'It's so hot!' he says.

The sun is starting to get low in the sky and the worst of the heat has passed. It's well past the time it'd take for Davy to come back with help too.

'This is how it is now,' I say. 'It's not specially hot today. Is you thirsty? If you want I can run ahead to the river and get some cold water for you.'

'No,' Phoenix says. Then he whispers, 'Don't leave,' but he's not saying it to me, he's saying it to all the empty broken windows in the buildings in the street around us, like the ghosts of his family is all up there, looking down on us.

'It'll be okay, Phoenix,' I say, coz I wanna say something kindly, but with no doctor coming up the road, with Davy and Alle deserting me, I dunno how it will be okay. Do I just convince Phoenix to come home to my place? What will Da say when I walk in with a boy wrapped in a blanket, who he's never seen before, who could be carrying some deadly disease?

'We'll rest at the river,' I say. 'I'll get you some nice cold water, and you can sit in the sun and let your bones defrost.'

He's walking kind of hunchbacked, like an old person walks, the wooden circle necklace he put on like he owned it swinging from side to side. He's not walking like a boy at all. I wish I thought to go back to Alle's kitchen and look for some food or something for Phoenix. He hasn't eaten for a hundred years. He must have a real ache in his belly.

I sit him at the top of the bridge next to the little posy that Alle made and scramble down the bank and fill up my water bottle for him. I drink my fill first, refill, then scramble back up the rocks beside the bridge.

Back on top, Phoenix is sitting there whistling to that cheeky raven like they's old pals. When I creep closer the raven sees me and takes off down the river making complaining noises that bounce off the water and echo for ages.

'Is that your friend?' I ask, half-joking.

'Eyes wide,' Phoenix says, and waves the wooden bird at me.

I lift my eyebrows at him and hand him the drink bottle.

He drinks and splutters and drinks some more like his throat muscles is surprised to have to swallow. 'Is this from the river?'

'Same river that's been feeding my township my whole life!' I say.

And he holds it to his eye and smiles. 'Clean.' Then he picks up the little bubble with the pretend snow in it from out of the arrangement Alle made in his posy. 'Ha,' he says, and shakes it and tilts his head.

The sun hits his scalp and the little hairs in the pores on his shaved head, they seem to be white where they's pushing up between the drawn-on blue lines, which is a surprise. He doesn't look like a person who'd have white hair. I think back to the photo. I'm pretty sure it was darker there.

'What colour was your hair when you had some?' I ask.

'Brown.' Phoenix runs his hand over the stubble on his head. The stubble that's definitely white. He hauls himself up and looks around, and then he points away down the river. The way the raven went. 'That way,' he says, sure as anything. He puts the pretend snow bubble on the top of the bridge rail and sets off.

'Did you know,' he calls back to me, his voice growing a little stronger and not so scratchy, 'that ravens point with their beaks? And they mimic other animals to get them to do what they want ...'

I'm definitely wondering if he was listening, listening, to someone calling the raven just now.

Then I'm just trailing behind as we climb down and follow the river out of the ruins. Me, glancing back to the bridge as often as I can for a chance to see Davy and the doctor crossing to look for me. So I can call them down here.

I don't see them. And I don't see them, and we's getting further away. And I don't see them and it's gonna be dark soon.

Phoenix knows what is happening. He can feel it in his bones. He thinks of Walter turning to dust. He thinks of the fairy stories of people dancing a night and coming out a hundred years later – they never lasted long, did they? It makes sense what is happening, he knew it as soon as he heard the whoosh of the doors unsealing.

He isn't scared by it. He just needs enough time to get to the bog is all. Enough time to make it back *home*. And then his body can do what it wants. Ashes to ashes, dust to dust, bog to bog. He can become part of everything, and everything can become part of him. He squeezes his mum's necklace and smiles.

Shelby is looking at him again. 'You don't look so good. Your skin's gone wrinkly. Probbly just from being in the water so long …'

But Phoenix knows it isn't that. 'I'm old. A hundred. A hundred and twelve.' And he starts laughing.

Shelby laughs too. 'I guess you is. I din't think of it like that.' Phoenix stops and turns to her. He isn't laughing anymore. 'My body. It's. I'm ...' He takes a moment. 'Ageing.' And then he stops talking and reaches into Shelby's pocket and pulls out a pinch of Walter's dust. 'Ashes to ashes.'

'What? You mean you're gonna turn to dust too? In front of me? You can't do that! I saved you! You's alive!'

Phoenix shrugs. His muscles are getting weaker, his bones feel empty and light, and when the wind blows he wonders if it might just up and blow him away. He thinks of Gran and his sisters. And the thought of being blown away on the wind with them fills him with warmth.

They don't say anything much after that. Shelby whistles once and points to his head, at the white hair that's sprouting, and growing down over his shoulders faster and faster, at the beard that's twisting from his chin. She looks scared. But she takes his arm when his back curves and his feet catch on the ground, and she doesn't pull away when a sore on his skin opens up and starts to pus and bleed. 'We're going a long way from the city,' she mumbles, but it's more to herself than to Phoenix. In the distance, Phoenix hears a train hoot, and smiles at how trains sound just the same even though a hundred years have passed.

Shelby freezes at the sound, though. 'What's that? Some kind of giant critter? I heard this last time I was near the river!' She scrambles up a nearby wall. Phoenix wants to tell her about trains, wants to find out what this world they are in is like, but it's all too hard. All too exhausting. And it isn't just his body ageing, either. Something's changing inside his head too. Memories and thoughts are getting harder to hold on to. Like they're already turning to ash.

He sits on an old stone wall to try to gather himself. He can't forget. He needs to get home to Mum. Needs to see if the seed he planted has grown. If he listened well enough to the Ravened Girl to give these people what they need. That gift of the seed from their most ancient ancestor – now he's an ancestor too. There's something in that thought that gives him energy. He just needs to get to the bog to show Shelby.

Shelby's up high standing on the wall yelling and pointing. 'It's a machine! A big machine like a bus, moving! What's it doing?' Phoenix can hardly concentrate on the string of questions that follow – he needs her to focus! – and when he gets up and trudges on, Shelby runs after him. 'Wait!' Shelby stops and bends down, poking at something on the ground. 'Looks like a drone,' she says. She circles it a few times, then takes another look. There is a parcel attached to the underside of it. Papers poke through the waxed box, aged and destroyed by time. Shelby reaches into the back of the parcel and pulls out a handful of paper. 'They's notices. I used to love these. But look at this date! This is from more than a year back!' She reads the one in her hand, her eyes turning wide as plates. 'Alle was right? Look!' Phoenix looks at the notice, squinting his eyes and rubbing away the watery film settling over the top.

'*KIND PEOPLE,*

Central government of the townships was set up as an aide to your autonomy, with a projected budget of one hundred years. It is a mark of your ability to remain self-sufficient that we have gone beyond our projected date for obsolescence. That time has now come.

Attached are maps of the other townships in your region. We suggest you get together and form local councils to share harvests, manage population and create plans for assisting the recovering land surrounding your townships. The government will hold annual summits for which you must send a representative to report on your progress and needs. Details of the summits are also attached.

Rail systems have been cleared and reutilised with solar trains to aid long-distance travel and freight transport.

Passenger drones will be repurposed for use by townships to assist with reunification. Local phone towers must now be serviced and powered by your townships.

We must never forget the lessons of the last one hundred years. We must teach our children and their children the value of living kindly and responsibly. We thank you for all the sacrifices you have made in your lifetimes to aid recovery. Go forth, and above all, go kindly upon this honoured earth.'

'Oh,' she says. 'We never got this message! Our township din't know. Our doctor din't know and she's the mayor. I gotta get this to her! She said people were leaving their townships, she was worried they wasn't good people, I think. Her phone wasn't working. But this changes everything, Phoenix! We'll be able to travel to the other seven hundreds. To the city. What's it like? To be free to go out there in the world? Is it scary?'

Phoenix takes her hand in his. He talks softly, barely more than a whisper, his memories bright in his words. 'There's so much! Castles. Rivers, mountains. Libraries, museums, forests. You can see it all.'

'Me?' Shelby asks. 'Me, travel to see sights like a storybook explorer? Phoenix, I never left my seven hundred before now, and you's like the third new person I ever met! I never even dreamed of this!'

'Start dreaming,' Phoenix says. 'You know what they say. You've got to jump from the cliff and grow wings on the way down.' He turns away, and keeps walking.

'Phoenix! I gotta get this to everyone!' she yells. 'Was that hooting machine a solar train?' But then she sighs loudly and runs to catch up. 'I gotta make sure we haven't released a great pandemic on the world and then I gotta tell them that everyone is walking bout and riding trains and that the phones is out coz we din't fix the tower electrics. Hey, I can go to the next township and talk to the egg farm girl there.' She stops and takes a deep breath. 'It's okay if you wanna say, "Shut up, Shelby, we gotta do this first!" My friend Davy, he'd be the one talking right now if he was here, and I'd say that to him.'

It's night by the time they reach the bog. The moon is a giant white ball, bigger and closer and clearer than Phoenix's ever seen it, lighting the bog up like day. He likes this new kindly world. He closes his eyes and listens to the night birds. Their calls are so loud and brilliant and beautiful and he can't help but howl out his own croaked song with them.

'No bones and ghosts then?' Shelby says, but she doesn't look convinced.

Phoenix smiles. 'Hi, Mum.' He wraps his arms around his mum's tree, grown so tall it towers high above them both. An old wooden bench covered over in vines hides beneath it. He smiles when he sees the five smaller trees, planted in an arc around his mum, and another tree with a sign nailed to a post in front of it. *Wolfy, our best friend for 22 years.* And he smiles even more at the tree so strange he knows for certain that it came from the Ravened Girl's bog seed, grown healthy and tall.

'That's a real big mama tree.' Shelby whistles between her teeth again. 'You know, my ma died too. Oh, I still got a da. So it's not like I'm alone. And I guess you're not either, coz here she is, mama tree.'

Phoenix holds Alle's picture up next to the tree. 'And here's your cure.'

Shelby's eyes grow wide. 'This one here? You're sure? This is the one?' She picks one of the peeling fruits with a nut emerging from the middle of it. A dark nut with a little whorl at the centre and a sprinkling of the brightest red you could ever see. 'Look. Like a fingerprint.' Phoenix nods, and hears the bones in his neck creak and crack with the effort of it.

'Here.' He hands Shelby his seed journal. His fingers find the carving on the bark of his mum's tree, grown up the trunk so far he almost misses it. He takes Shelby's fingers and runs them over the carving. 'This is a message from ... our ancestors.' It is getting harder than ever to talk. His voice comes out in raspy puffs like the whisper of wind through branches.

'What's it say?'

Phoenix shrugs. 'I don't know.'

Shelby runs her fingers over the carving again and scrunches her face tight, like she's making sure she's remembering the shape of them just right, and then she hugs the seed journal tight to her chest.

Phoenix reaches into Shelby's pockets and takes out the dust from Walter. He sprinkles it all around their mum's tree and in between all the other memory-orial trees growing up around her. 'Pinkie promise,' he whispers, and blows the last of the dust from his palm into the hollow. He takes Splinky and nestles him inside the hollow too.

'What bout you?' Shelby says. 'We can get you help now we have the seed. The doctor ...'

Phoenix squeezes her hand. 'I'm home,' he says. 'Thank you, Shelby Jones.' From far away, there is the rumble of thunder. Rain patters down on their heads and shoulders. 'Eyes wide, Shelby,' Phoenix whispers. 'Eyes wide.'

I stand in the rain gripping the seed journal and the cure seed as Phoenix smiles at me, then hitches his blanket around himself, kicks off his slippers, wiggles his toes in the mud and wades into the bog, the wooden raven pressed tight to his chest. He just stands there looking like he's waiting for something.

I stay standing under the mama tree, right next to the tree with the strange little nuts that will save us. The mama tree has my name carved on it. That's what I saw anyway, and what I felt with my fingers, felt in my bones. A carved zigzag lightning bolt next to a carved two-branch tree next to a straight-up-and-down tick. *SFJ*, carved straight and jaggy, ᛋᚠ✓. 'Eyes wide, Shelby,' I say.

'Phoenix?' I tuck the journal up under my shirt to keep it dry. The thunder is a worry. Wild storms can whip up suddenly, and this is low land. If there's a flash flood we could be in trouble.

'Remember! *Hands, Face, Space*,' Phoenix says, and smiles, his face ghostly in the moonlight, and I nod and tear off the bottom of my T-shirt to use as a mask for when I see the others. I really hope this cure comes quick. Or my super rare blood has saved me. I don't wanna be apart from everyone for long. I tie it across my face.

'Phoenix, how did things get so bad in your time? How did you pollute even the skies? Miss Drinkwater says you all thought it din't matter what you did, that the earth would keep giving air you could breathe and water you could drink and dirt you could grow things in, but that wasn't true.'

Phoenix don't turn back, ankle-deep in mud and moon-shimmery water. My voice is a bit muffled by the shirt cloth tied over my face, but I think he can hear me.

'You was just a kid. There's not much you can do bout the world you's born into, I guess, cept try to walk real gentle where you can and give voice to the critters that's too quiet to be heard and be a different kind of adult when you grow up, but you never did get to grow up.' He ain't listening, so I mutter, 'Inna hundred years, you din't get to grow up.'

I go climb a little up the bank and tuck in under the mama tree on the bench out of the rain, trying not to step in any of the Walter dust. I know in my head it's just dust, but in my heart I think it's Phoenix's little brother. So I don't dare breathe for worry of sucking in *the* Walter Ticerat through my T-shirt mask.

Walter and all the dead children was the reason our great grandparents left the cities, left the modern world and went to the seven hundred townships. This is why they named a school after him, probbly. He was the first person who got the ancient virus given back to us by a ravaged land. His sickness caused people to stop and think bout what really matters.

He was the boy who changed the world.

Phoenix is still just a white-haired, white-blanket shape standing in the moonlight. Will he really just dissolve to dust like Walter? I wanna see if there's lights back towards the city, torches of Da and Davy looking for me maybe. I'm gonna be in so much trouble. I also wonder where that honking machine went. It must be a solar train like the newsletter says. A train!

I dunno why there's a train out here. If there's a train, there has to be people too. What would people be doing on a train? Where is there to go? It's a strange idea to not stay on our seven hundred and wait like we's s'posed to.

I wish someone from our place had seen the train. I wish they knew what to make of it. I don't. Have some of the seven hundreds already started taking back the old world? Is that allowed?

I sit down and wait, coz I'm trapped here now, ain't I? I can't leave Phoenix standing ankle-deep in the bog looking off across it, like he's a frog bout to slide in and swim up the white river of moonlight that's wobbling on the surface water. I can't navigate my way all the way home just in the moonlight.

So I sit, and watch Phoenix, trying to keep my eyes wide, and think bout Daisy and Joe waiting to get approval for a baby, bout Da secretly wanting a partner but not wanting to get my hopes up, and our teacher wanting for a younger teacher to take her place. Can we have all that now? Is everything set to change? Oh, Davy's gonna be so excited bout being allowed to rummage through the city for bits and pieces!

Phoenix down there, a ghost in the moonlight. A child when the world fell apart, and me, a child that sees it all back together.

He's right. He don't belong here. There's been kids like both of us lived and died between our times. So many things changed to get from his world to mine, and now things look like they's changing once more. Change is scary. That's what it is. Scary. But we changed to make this honoured earth better, and maybe changing again to leaving our seven hundreds will make our lives better. We's good people. We's kind people. We will be careful.

I tuck the seed book up against the tree, kick off my boots and wade into the bog beside Phoenix. The water swirls round my ankles like there's some swamp critter swimming around down there, pushing through the honoured mud. Whatever's down there deep in the swamp has been waiting a long time for us. Her kindly nudges against the soles of my feet tell me we's welcome. Like she knows us.

'Okay?' I whisper to Phoenix.

He takes the deepest breath and sighs.

'Can you hear? Her singing?' he says, his voice crackling like old paper, and he turns his head to the side like he's listening, and smiles. He's old now. His skin and bones is sagging and his hair shines white. His eyes is wet and shimmer in the moonlight like they's made of the surface of the bog. In the letter his friend asked if when he dies he wants to be sunk down deep in the bog, become a part of it. I feel like he's already partway there, just dissolving into the water and moonlight.

I stand with him a while, just so he's not alone, until the soles of my feet tingle and my toes ache from the chill.

A girl is singing. She's a long way away and I can't make out her words, but her voice is light and floaty like the misting rain. It trails in on the night sky. 'I hear her!' I whisper and stand and listen until my feet is too cold to stay there.

'Go kindly,' I whisper and wrap my hands around Phoenix's wrinkly bony ones and squeeze. His head dips in the moonlight. The tiniest nod, but I get the feeling Phoenix is so far away now that he might already be back in the past.

'Pinkie promise,' he whispers.

I go sit in the dry under the mama tree, the tree with my initials like I was always gonna end up here, and wait to see what Phoenix does next.

A train toots far off and a dog comes romping through the trees, the moonlight through the leaves making patches of bright on his brown fur. He stops and stares at me and I stare back. He's followed by a small boy who comes right up to the dog and stops and stares at me too. Are they real? The moonlight patches are the only things that move on his small round face. Then he smiles, the dog wags his tail and they's off again.

Three girls come bundling down the path after them. They's a hand-holding, shoving, skipping, giggling, chattering mess of girls. There's at least three conversations going at once! I wait for them to see me.

'Walter Ticerat, you stop right there!' one of them yells, making little Walter laugh. The oldest girl comes over to me, leans down and for a moment her face looks so familiar I almost think I recognise her. She's the dead spit of the young photo of my mother that Da keeps beside his bed from when both of them met at sixteen. Then she smiles at me and catches up to the other girls.

Following the wild bunch of girls is Phoenix, young healthy Phoenix with dark hair, following a step behind and watching out for Walter just the same as the girls is doing. Then he sees me, he comes over and bends down, his face close to mine, but I feel like he's looking through me. He's not looking at me at all like the oldest girl did. His dark eyes go right through to something behind me.

He reaches out, right through my shoulder, and I lean back, but still the cold of his fingers drives into my body, icy trails spreading down my arm. Then he stands and pulls. Another hand is holding his, another arm follows. A woman behind me laughs and stands up right through me, leaving all of me icy cold and gasping. She wraps an arm around Phoenix, gives him a gentle squeeze and they walk away following the path of the girls, Walter and the dog, down along the trail twisting through the bog. That's not a real trail. I'm not following them down there!

I don't think Phoenix saw me at all. I think maybe he just saw his mother. Is this a different time when they was all alive? Is this what it's like when a place holds memories of times before? Which of us is the ghost?

Then Phoenix turns back, looks right at me this time, smiles and waves.

I wave too, but lose sight of them all as they dance and chatter into a mist hovering above the swamp. Little yellow lights floating away is the last I see. The noise of them fades and I'm alone again.

Next thing I know, someone is shaking me. 'Shelby! Shelby Jones, is you alive or what?'

It's light and Davy is leaned over me red-faced, sweaty and looking scared. 'Davy!' I say, really excited to be back in my time again. 'You found me! Wait! Don't get too close!' I pull the T-shirt-cloth back up over my mouth and nose.

But Davy's too busy grinning. 'I wouldn't give up looking. I saw how you moved that snow bubble up to the bridge top to point the way, so I headed down beside the river! I heard a strange noise, a honking noise like a giant goose. You'll never guess what it was! But whatcha doing all the way out here?' he asks. 'And what d'ya mean, don't get too close?'

'The train,' I say. 'Oh!' I leap up. 'Phoenix!'

Morning mist rises off the bog, billowing and moving, and in all that white and water and tall rushes and clumpy grass, there's something whiter. A white blanket out in the bog. He's fallen and drowned while I was sleeping. Did pollution gases get to him?

I run. 'Davy! That's Phoenix, help!'

Davy splashes behind me. I drop down into the watery mud beside the blanket. My heart's thumping at my ears. My hand fights me reaching to lift the sopping blanket, terrified of what might be underneath. A grey water-swollen dead boy looking like an old man is what I'm specting, but there's nothing there! Water, weeds, a cloudy puff of mud.

I plunge my hands in, feeling through water and weeds. My fingers catch on a leathery string. It's the necklace with the wooden ring on it, the one he was wearing.

I jump up and look around, still specting to find Phoenix floating nearby. I splash off in a big circle, looking. 'Can you see him?' I ask, waving the necklace to prove he was here.

But he's not lying anywhere we can see. There's no current to float him away. It's still. Dead still.

Mud sucks at my feet, so I stagger back to the blanket, press my hands into the cold stringy mud there, feeling around for fabric, for bone, looking for dust floating like what Walter turned into. Nothing.

Phoenix has gone. I thought that was just me dreaming him happily going off with his family? Or was it real? Did Phoenix really find a way back to his time?

Or maybe that's what happens when you die. You exist in your happiest memories and in the dreams people have of you. Like Phoenix's friend said in the letter. I swish the weeds off the necklace and pull it over my head.

'Who? Was it one of them frozen kids?' Davy asks. 'Is you sick now? Is that why I can't come close?'

'He defrosted and came alive,' I say, 'and we walked all night to get here, coz this is where he lived, but he was ageing, Davy. Ageing like his body knew how old it was really, and then he just went into the bog, wearing this.' I touch the wet wood necklace.

I look around one last time. I feel like wherever he went he's okay now. He's back with the ones who love him.

'The swamp?' Davy asks.

'He called it a bog,' I say. I point to the slippers left beside the bog, the blood inside them washed out to pink in the rain. 'He just kicked off his slippers calm as anything and walked right in!'

Something hard prods my toes, and I feel down and pull up the carved bird Phoenix took into the water with him. There's something bout the shape of the beak, something bout its pale eyes looking at me. I take the tree nut from my pocket, push it into the bird's beak, where it fits perfectly like it was made for it, and then use my heel to push them both deep into the mud.

Phoenix worked so hard to get the seed to me. He carried this bird all the way down here. It should go with him to wherever. It belongs to the bog.

'Girl!' Da yells like he never learned my name.

'Da!' I call, and wave at him running down the hill. I wade back out of the swamp, and run at him. 'Stop! You can't touch me!' I tell him even though I want nothing more than to be hugged by my da in that warm flannel shirt that stinks of chickens and sweat.

'I'm sorry, I had to try to help them!' I say.

'You should have come and told us,' Da says.

'Is the doctor there now?' I ask. 'Is she helping them?'

'The doctor and a man called Alle are burying them now. They're being real careful and wearing proper suits like you should've done and going over every single surface with a full spray and scrub! And come tomorrow they're going to set the pod room and lab up in flames just to be sure nothin' is left of it. Those kids are all more dead than alive. The doctor says they never found a cure. None of those children would ever have been able to be regenerated after this long.'

'But Phoenix did,' I say. 'He woke and he came down here to where his family once lived.'

Da looks around. 'Where's this Phoenix?' he asks. 'Did you touch him? Did you catch the virus?'

'We's got the cure.' I point to the tree. 'Well, kinda almost got the cure, it's in its honoured seed.' I run and pull a peeling pod off the tree and point to the nut. 'Alle worked it all out. Maybe don't burn the lab just yet. He just din't know where to find this tree. And Phoenix …'

I point out to the blanket. Da kicks off his boots and wades out to where the blanket is sinking into the muddy water. He lifts it out of the water with a stick, not getting too close to the blanket all sopping and dripping, then looks all around.

'Where, girl?' he calls.

I shrug. I dunno how to say that I think he sank into the bog and somehow returned to his family. Last I saw him was in a maybe-dream and he looked so happy.

Da sighs and wades back to me. 'Are you sure it was a frozen kid, not one of those kids from the fields over the hill we saw?' He peers through the mist.

'I helped Phoenix wake up and helped him all the way here,' I say. 'He was definitely a frozen kid, but I don't think he's here anymore. I think he's gone and sunk in the bog or something overnight. And I might have the virus now too. Even though my blood is the best. I can't come home with you until we know if I'm sick!'

Da pulls a long white stick thing out of his pocket. 'Dr Geraldine made us go back and get it from her house the moment she saw the open capsules. They never found the cure, but they did work out a test. All we need is a prick of your bestest blood, girl, and we'll know how much trouble you've got yourself into.'

I hold my breath while Da sticks me with the biggest needle I ever seen. He watches the numbers. I can't breathe. I don't wanna die! I'm too young! What if Alle can't really make the cure from the tree seeds or it takes months to create a medicine?

Da's staring at that stick hard as me, and his face goes all stiff. 'Shelby Frankie Jones,' he says.

He never uses my name! This is terrible! I'm done for!

'I'm sorry to say there's a lot of chores waiting for you

back home. You're fit as a mule!' And then his face cracks into the biggest grin ever. 'No virus in you, girl. Now come give me that hug.'

I rip the cloth from my face and hug Da tight around the middle, breathing in his old chicken-farmer stink. Then I hug Davy too.

'Da? Did you really see people? Just wandering around? It's true?' I pull a newsletter from my pocket and show him the message the drone din't deliver. 'This says we can leave but the next township is hundreds of kilometres away, isn't it?'

'It is! I read it,' Da says, patting the paper in his pocket. 'It's very exciting news! I can't wait to get these newsletters back to our township. This is why the phone stopped working. We didn't know we were meant to keep the towers serviced. Your friend Alle has a lot of science skills. The doctor is gonna bring him back to our township for things like fixing the phone tower and teaching science at the school.'

'He's wild about science. A bit too wild! But he'll probbly like that,' I say. 'He really likes kids and I think he musta got real lonely living in a lab so long. Everything's changing! New people!'

Davy jumps up and down. 'We saw them!' he yells.

'We saw a real live train rolling along the old rusty rails, and people beside the rails left their rows of crops, bringing spades and wiping hands on aprons, and walked to the train waving. And some jumped aboard! The train had people sitting in its carriage, waving out open windows and doors, and a man threw down a few sacks of wheat or something to a man who was waiting, and there was kids too! Almost as many as our whole school even!'

Da nods. 'It seems the rails have brought them to the river valley to grow crops and maybe scavenge some building materials from the old city? The doctor says the townships government just stopped communicating last year. She was afraid if she told us we'd panic bout medications and stuff and worry bout people coming to our seven hundred to steal our food, but it looks to me like the townships government just handed everything over to a national government and the other townships don't need to steal from us. According to the newsletter, we're meant to be sending people out to the national government to organise what we need.'

'Oh.' I run to where I was lying and point to Phoenix's seed diary. 'Phoenix had this. It's full of seeds.'

Da picks it up and turns the chunky pages slowly. Each page has writing and pictures and a lumpy little envelope stuck on it.

'Shelby!' Da says. 'This book has seventeen varieties of apples, and black plums, dragonfruit, jackfruit and oh … look at this, a tamarillo! This is a real national treasure. Nashi pears and – aww, the pomegranate packet is missing. I would've liked to try a pomegranate.'

I point over the hill. 'I have a feeling Alle gave it to the people you saw, or tied it in a posy for them to find, or something. He calls them the pomegranates. He says they salvage stuff from the edge of the city. Maybe they bring pomegranates to him for payment? I saw he had some fruit that looked like it might be a pomegranate.'

Dad shuts the book carefully. 'My tongue can't hardly wait. We'll be egg farmers *and* exotic fruit farmers, my girl.' Then he looks at me and Davy.

'Well, my wayward kids, do we go to the top of the hill to see what's happening with those people and their train, or do we get this lot back to the doctor right now?'

Davy nods furiously, eyes wide. 'Like my great Grandy Charlie used to say, best thing to do is jump from the cliff and grow wings on the way down! Let's go now!'

'I'm so starving my belly is sticking to my backbone,' I say. 'But even I wanna go up the hill!'

Da smiles. 'Alright, just quickly, up and back. The doctor will want to know what they're doing and probbly come with us for a first meeting, but we gotta rush all this stuff to Dr Geraldine and Alle so they don't dismantle the lab, and make sure we're all clear to get home in time to shut the chickens in. Davy's mas can't be neglecting their farm for ours.'

'Maybe you'll find a partner from over the hill to come back with us?' I ask.

Da laughs. 'That's not how it works, girl. Ya can't just be waving at someone from a hilltop one minute and taking them home the next. Partners ain't pomegranates.'

I laugh too. 'And we need a new teacher, and a couple of mules …'

'Or we could have a mule for a teacher!' Davy says, setting off up the next hill ahead of us. 'Could've taught you a lesson bout digging your heels in and staying put when we's coming to rescue you!'

'Hee haw!' I call.

'Hee haw!' a raven calls from high in the big mama tree at the edge of the swamp.

I stop and look back, then yell into the swamp. 'It was nice to meet you, Phoenix Ticerat. Go kindly upon this honoured earth!'

$\mathcal{S}$lowly, slowly. The sky above is lightening. The stars disappear, one by one. And the wild whispers of all that has been, and all that is yet to come, swirls and swarms, filling the sky in bursts of bees and streaking stars, in howling winds and padding paws, in ragged claws and storied rocks, in footsteps taken and hands held, in dreams and wonders they whisper ... *Eyes wide. Eyes wide.*

Can you hear them? Can you?

Listen ...

ACKNOWLEDGEMENTS

Zana: There are always so many wonderful people in the writing community that make writing books possible, but I have never before had a writing experience like this one. Huge thanks to the extremely talented Bren MacDibble, whose work I have always admired, and who made writing a book together feel like joyful play. Every moment was a delight – from our frantic flights of plotting, to the edits made wonderfully easy by having another brain who not only knows the book as intimately as I do, but who extended and encouraged me to take the ideas to a whole other level – Bren, this was an absolute delight and I loved every moment.

Thanks also to my ever-supportive agent Claire Wilson at RCW, and the fantastic team at Allen & Unwin. And an especially big thank you to Ginny Grant, Sucheta Raj, Hilary Reynolds and Jodie Webster for falling in love with this and helping it become.

As always, to the community of writers, readers, librarians, booksellers, teachers and tellers of tales – thank you for your stories, inspiration and support. I couldn't do this without you.

And to my family – Mina, Mischa, Luca and Jugs – you are everything to me.

Bren: It's telling that the only manuscript I completed in the dreadful first years of COVID-19 was a joint project. So massive thanks to Zana for suggesting a collaboration, for bringing an absolute wealth of knowledge and ideas to this story, for the wild creative chats and for being such a joy. Thanks also to Ginny, Sucheta, Hilary, Jodie and the Allen & Unwin team for embracing tough topics, bringing this all together and making the dream real. And to Jo for your amazing moody cover, I adore those colours. Thanks to my readers and those who champion children's literature. The support you've given me in the last few years means everything.

ABOUT THE AUTHORS

 **Bren MacDibble** was raised on farms all over New Zealand. She backpacked the world in her twenties, stopped off in Australia on the way home and stayed. She lived in Melbourne for twenty years, then travelled Australia living and working in a bus, and now runs holiday villas on the stunning coral coast of Western Australia. Her first books, *How to Bee* (2017) and *The Dog Runner* (2019), won multiple awards including a Children's Book Council of Australia Book of the Year and New Zealand Book Awards. *Across the Risen Sea* (2020) was also shortlisted for multiple awards and nominated for a CILIP Carnegie Medal. All three novels are 'eco-fiction' adventures, set in an imaginary climate-changed world. Bren hopes that her stories give her readers courage and the language to talk about the future they'd like to see.

Bren's novels are published in the UK by Old Barn Books, in paperback and as eBooks. Reading resources are available to download from our website. **www.macdibble.com**

Also by Bren MacDibble and available from Old Barn Books:

HOW TO BEE

Nine year-old Peony dreams of becoming the best 'bee' the farm has ever seen, scrambling through the fruit trees to pollinate by hand with feather wands. She has love, she has food and if she could just become a 'bee' she'd be super-cherries happy. But her mother wants her to live in the city, where all the fruit is sent. Torn between two different worlds, Peony fights to protect her family and the world she loves.

Quirky, original and heartfelt, this is an all too plausible dystopian adventure, exploring themes of family loyalty and the environment' –The Bookseller

THE DOG RUNNER
Nominated for the Carnegie Medal

Ella and her brother, Emery, are alone in a city that's starving to death. If they are going to survive, they must get away, up-country, to find Emery's mum. But how can two kids travel such big distances across a dry, barren and dangerous landscape? They hitch their five big doggos to their dry-land dogsled and go mushing. But when Emery is injured, Ella must find a way to navigate them through rough terrain, and even rougher encounters with desperate people.

The Dog Runner is a tense, thrilling adventure story full of close calls and peril, but it's also glowing with heart... The all-too timely reminders about the importance of the environment and food security, Bren MacDibble's distinctive writing style, and the delicious sense of threat make The Dog Runner hard to resist.' –Booktrust

ACROSS THE RISEN SEA
Nominated for the Carnegie Medal

Neoma and Jag and their small community are 'living gentle lives' on high ground surrounded by the risen sea. When strangers from the Valley of the Sun arrive unannounced, the two friends find themselves drawn into a web of secrecy and lies that endangers their whole way of life.

A bold, clear-headed call of a possible future world, beyond climate disaster and pandemic. It offers humanity options, from trade and politics, to community, bartering and practical skills. Hope, menace, mistrust and wisdom lie in this bruised future...It leaves us all with an urge to 'go gently" –Bookwagon blog

Zana Fraillon is an internationally acclaimed, multi-award winning author of books for children and young adults. Her work has been published in over fifteen countries and is in development for both stage and screen. Zana was born in Melbourne, but spent her early childhood in San Francisco. She is a three-time Carnegie-nominated author, and her 2016 novel *The Bone Sparrow* won the ABIA Book of the Year for Older Children, The Readings Young Adult Book Prize, the Amnesty CILIP Honour, and was chosen as the IBBY Honour Book to represent Australian children's literature. Her other books, which include *The Ones That Disappeared* (2017) and *The Lost Soul Atlas* (2020), have also won multiple awards, including the New South Wales Literary Award and the Aurealis Award. Zana now lives in Melbourne with her husband, three children and two dogs, and is currently undertaking a PhD at La Trobe University. **www.zanafraillon.com**

This is the first time that Old Barn Books has had the honour of publishing Zana's work and we are thrilled to be able to bring her voice to our list in this stunning duet with Bren. We hope this won't be the last time they work together!